He was undeni

He was also, Meg
undeniably contemp

Even casually dressed, he stood out in the
crowd—as he would stand out in any crowd. He
was grinning, his eyes crinkled, his sensual
mouth slanted crookedly.

He was a heartbreaker. Tempting as sin itself...

An odd, jellying sensation quivered deep inside
her as she faced up to the fact that this
devastatingly attractive man was the father of
her child...

And he knew nothing about it.

Grace Green grew up in Scotland but later emigrated to Canada with her husband and children. They settled in 'Beautiful Natural BC' and now live in a house just minutes from ocean, beaches, mountains and rainforest. Grace makes no secret of her favourite occupation—her bumper sticker reads: 'I'D RATHER BE WRITING ROMANCE!' She also enjoys walking the sea wall, gardening, getting together with other authors...and watching her characters come to life, because she knows that once they do they'll take over and write her stories for her.

Recent titles by the same author:

HIS UNEXPECTED FAMILY
NEW YEAR...NEW FAMILY

THE FATHERHOOD SECRET

BY
GRACE GREEN

To Sandy, Jilly and Grant
In memory of the Miltonduff years

All the characters in this book have no existence outside the imagination of the author, and have no relation whatsoever to anyone bearing the same name or names. They are not even distantly inspired by any individual known or unknown to the author, and all the incidents are pure invention.

First published in Great Britain 1999
Harlequin Mills & Boon Limited,
Eton House, 18-24 Paradise Road, Richmond, Surrey TW9 1SR

© Grace Green 1999

ISBN 0 263 81557 9

Set in Times Roman 10½ on 11¼ pt.
02-9904-52814 C1

Printed and bound in Norway
by AIT Trondheim AS, Trondheim

CHAPTER ONE

MEG was lounging on the window seat in her sister's bedroom, watching idly as her sister sewed one last lacy rose to the hem of her ivory wedding dress, when the sound of a powerful engine growled into the quiet August afternoon.

She glanced outside and was just in time to see a black Infiniti draw up in the driveway next door. Its sleek bodywork was veiled in dust, its windscreen spattered with dead bugs. Out-of-town guests, she reflected, here for the wedding. But a few days early...

She yawned lazily. "Dee, the Carradines have visitors."

The only response was the clatter of clothes hangers as her sister hung her dress in the closet.

"And wealthy," Meg added. "If their car's anything to go by! Do you know anybody who has a black—"

The driver's door opened and a man emerged. He turned toward the ocean and stretched out his arms as if to ease kinked muscles. He was tall, with a thatch of dark hair, a runner's lean build, a confident tilt to his head—

Meg gasped.

"Honey?" Deirdre came up behind her. "What's the matter? Oh, *dear!*" She made an unhappy tsking sound. "He's come early. James told me his best man wasn't going to arrive till the eve of the wedding. Meg, I'm so sorry. I know how difficult this is going to be for you."

"He's alone." Meg's voice trembled. "I thought his wife was coming, too."

"Alix will probably turn up closer to the time...she's

5

in the Middle East right now. I...saw her on the TV news last night. She's covering the war in..."

But Meg wasn't listening. She was too busy looking at Sam Grainger. She hadn't set eyes on the man for more than thirteen years...but just the sight of him had made her skin cold and clammy, despite the warmth of the summer day.

He turned slightly, and she jerked back behind the curtain. But he didn't look up. He hefted a bag from the trunk of his car and slammed the trunk shut. He started walking toward the house...and then, as if he'd suddenly changed his mind, strode back to the car. Opening the door, he tossed the bag in and walked away from the house—across the sidewalk, across the wide deserted street, over the salt grass above the beach, and down onto the beach itself.

"He's going for a walk," Deirdre said in a low voice, as they watched him shrug off his charcoal-gray suit jacket and thumb-hook it over his right shoulder. "Probably exhausted from his drive, and wanting a breath of ocean air."

Meg's gaze skimmed past the beach to the surging waves of the Pacific. Today, as on most days, the breeze was lively. Herrings gulls soared, white sails speckled the silver-blue water, and a handful of wind-surfers added the odd splash of vivid color.

A perfect picture postcard.

From their old family home on the outskirts of town, at the very end of Seaside Lane, Meg and Dee had a wonderful view of the crescent-shaped bay: three miles to the south jutted Cape Hamilton, with the Seashore Inn nestled in its sheltering embrace; to the north, the small town followed the curve of the sandy beach to Matlock's Marina, where moored yachts bobbed alongside narrow wooden jetties.

It was a view Meg had always treasured; but today

that view was marred by the tall figure striding along the sand in his elegant white shirt and snazzy city pants!

"Meg." Dee touched her arm. "You know we're supposed to go next door tonight, for Elsa's barbecue, but you don't *have* to if—"

"I can't hide from the man forever," Meg said. "Better to get that first meeting over with. At least Andy isn't here." She ran shaky fingers through the silky strands of her cropped honey-blond hair. "I have a few more days to brace myself for *that* horrendous meeting!"

"Do you think Sam will...?" Dee bit her lip, gazed anxiously into her sister's troubled blue eyes.

"Spot any resemblance?" Meg grimaced. "I doubt it. No one else ever has! The facial features are so different. Andy's a Stafford—he takes after our family in looks— except for the black hair and his build—and of course—" her laugh was without mirth "—his smile."

"Yes, he does have his father's smile. But Andy's more into scowling than smiling these days," Dee added hopefully. "Since he turned twelve he's become...well, you know!"

"Dee, I'm going after him."

"But the cadet campsite's a hundred miles from here and—"

"I'm going after *Sam.* It'll be better...safer...if we have our first meeting alone. Other people—James, his mother—might notice my...awkwardness. If I can get that initial contact over with, I'll feel more in control of the situation." She rose from the cushioned bench.

"Do you want me to come with you? I will, if—"

"Thanks, but this is something I need to do alone." Meg tucked her baggy white T-shirt into the waistband of her faded blue jogging pants, scooped her white cotton sun hat from the window seat, and made for the door.

"Aren't you going to change? Put on some makeup?"

Meg snorted contemptuously as she planted the wide-brimmed sun hat squarely on her head. "If there's one man in the world I'm not interested in impressing," she tossed over her shoulder as she stomped out, "it's Sam Grainger!"

You're a failure!

Sam Grainger winced, and pressed a hand against his temple in an attempt to quell the persistently lingering words of self-analysis that had battered his brain nonstop on the drive up from Portland to this sea-salty little town in the northwest corner of Washington State.

There was no getting away from it, though, because it was the truth: he was a failure and his life was empty. He was going to be forty in two months...and what did he have to show for it? He had no wife, no kids, no home...

No joy.

His lips twisted grimly as he tugged off his silk tie, shoved it in the hip pocket of his gray slacks, worked open the top button of his shirt. The only thing he had left—apart from the family firm which had been thrust upon him last year on his father's death—was his job. Divorce lawyer. And if *that* wasn't ironic, he didn't know what was.

He walked right to the edge of the water and let the sound of the ocean wash over him. The tide was going out. He almost wished he could go out with it. How easy it would be, to follow it, to—

"Hi!"

For a moment, he thought he'd imagined the voice. He didn't turn. But then a dog—a golden retriever—splashed into the sea just ahead of him, spattering a spray of salt water over his trousers.

He stifled the irritation he felt at having been disturbed. And turned.

A young woman—a teenager?—was standing a few

feet away, regarding him steadily from under the wide floppy brim of a white sun hat. He hadn't heard her approach, because of the surf's thunder.

There was something oddly defensive about her demeanor: though her blue eyes were shadowed by the hat's floppy brim, they had a wary gleam. And her unpainted lips were tightly set together, her hands punched into the pockets of her baggy jogging pants. Well, what the hell did she want? This was one huge beach! If she was afraid of strangers, why didn't she keep away from him?

"Hi," he said abruptly. The dog pranced out of the ocean and shook itself energetically, sending an arc of cold droplets over his trousers and shirt. He glanced again at the girl. Her cheeks had become pink.

"Sorry," she murmured. "A neighbor's dog...followed me along the beach—"

He made a curt dismissive gesture. "No harm done."

His mind was already on other matters. He'd better get back. The Carradines would probably have noticed his car in the drive, would be wondering what was going on. He should have let them know he was coming early, but when he'd left the courthouse, all he could think of was getting out of the city. And once on the highway, he hadn't wanted to stop.

"Enjoy your walk." He strode around the girl, giving her a wide berth. She seemed so tense...he didn't want to give her any cause for alarm...

But his last glimpse of her told him he hadn't succeeded. Her big blue eyes had frozen wide open—with shock, and some other emotion he couldn't absolutely define.

It had *looked* like anger, he reflected as he made his way back; but of course it couldn't have been. He and the girl were total strangers to each other—she could have no reason in the world to feel any hostility toward him!

Maybe she was high on something—or maybe she was just a bit wacky; one sandwich short of a picnic, as the saying went. Either way, he had no desire to run into her again!

And with that last abstracted thought, he wiped the bizarre encounter from his mind.

"I can't *believe* it, Dee!" Meg paced the kitchen furiously as she sputtered the words out. "He didn't even *remember* me! The man didn't even *know* me! I've spent the last thirteen years thinking about him—about his callousness, about the cavalier way he treated me, about—"

"Honey, I know." Dee opened the oven door to take out the dinner rolls she'd baked, and a gust of heat blasted into the already stiflingly hot kitchen. "But don't you think that's the best thing? If he doesn't even remember you, then when he sees Andy it's not going to occur to him, even remotely, that the boy could be his son!"

Meg jerked to a halt and glared at her sister. "I've already thought of that! But it just makes me boiling mad that as far as Sam Grainger's concerned, I'm so—so—"

"Forgettable?" Dee offered quietly.

Meg felt tears smart behind her eyes. She rubbed her knuckles over them belligerently. "Yes." Her sigh was heavy and filled with anger, frustration, pain. "Yes, I guess that's it." She managed a self-derisive smile. "My pride's hurt. It stings, dammit!"

Dee transferred the buns to a wire rack on the countertop. She didn't speak again till she was finished. "I have a feeling," she said carefully, "that his coming here will turn out to be the best thing that could have happened...as far as you're concerned. You've always

dreaded the day you might see him again, now it's here
and you got through that first meeting. I agree that the
way he treated you thirteen years ago was shameful—''

"To put it mildly!"

"—But Meg, you have to let it go. All men aren't
like Sam Grainger. You can't let what happened with
him taint the rest of your life, put you off men forever.''

"Jack was no better!" Meg retorted bitterly.

"But you got over Jack. Whereas, with Sam Gr—''

"How can I get over Sam Grainger? How can I ever
forget him, when every time I look at Andy—'' She
threw her hands up, unable to find the words to vent her
anguish and despair.

The grandfather clock out in the hall chimed six.

Dee clucked frustratedly. "Heavens, look at the time!
Meg, we're going to have to talk about this later. We'll
have to get dressed now, or we'll be late for the barbecue.''

Meg gave a weary nod. "You use the shower first,"
she said. "I'll clean up in here."

As Dee left the kitchen, Meg moved over to the sink,
the wide sill above it cluttered with seashells and potted
geraniums and several hastily scrawled postcards from
Andy. From the window, she could see across the white
picket fence to the Carradines's backyard.

Walking along the path in Elsa's rose garden were the
three elderly Barnley sisters, her permanent boarders.

On the patio, James was dragging Elsa's two cedar
picnic tables together. Both were set for dinner.

Elsa must have invited a crowd.

Thank goodness for that, Meg reflected tautly as she
turned away. The more people, the better. It would make
it easier for her to avoid Sam Grainger.

"I should've called you before leaving Portland, Mrs C.
I didn't mean to create a problem—''

"No problem, Sam." Elsa Carradine raised her warm brown gaze from the lemon cheesecake she was trimming and smiled at Sam who was leaning against the kitchen countertop, one tanned hand wrapped around a can of beer. "I'll ask Dee to put you up for the next two or three days till the painter and carpet man finish in the guest room."

"She won't mind?"

"Heavens, no. She's the most hospitable person on the face of this earth! The Staffords just have the three bedrooms—Dee uses the fourth as her sewing room, she's a dressmaker by trade, you remember?—but she can give you Andy's room—he's going to be away till the eve of the wedding and by that time, your room here will be habitable."

Before Sam could ask who Andy was, the screen door swung open and James came in from the yard. Tall and thin, with graying brown hair and his mother's brown eyes, he was a quiet man with a keen mind and a quirky sense of humor. He and Sam had met and become close friends in their first year at university and though their paths had diverged after they graduated from law school, they had never lost touch.

He had been Sam's best man when Sam had married Alix; now he was returning the honor.

"Right, Ma!" He crossed to the fridge. "Tables are set. Barbecue's lit. Time for a beer." He helped himself to a can, and popped it open. "Nobody's arrived yet?"

As if on cue, the doorbell rang.

"I'll get it." Elsa whisked off her frilly apron. "You boys go on outside."

As James ushered Sam out to the patio, he said, "How long is it since you've seen Dee?"

"Must be...oh, maybe sixteen years. I didn't see her when I came to town thirteen years ago—"

"No, you stayed at the Seashore Inn...and you were

there for only the one night. That was an awful time for you! What a helluva thing to happen—I often think about it, and now that I have Dee, I wonder how I'd have coped if I'd been in your shoes. To hear such news and then—''

The screen door opened, putting an end to their conversation. Elsa brought out the first of the guests, the Fairchilds, a middle-aged couple who lived down the street.

Then from the bottom of the garden tottered the twittery Barnley sisters, who had been boarding with Elsa for the last ten years, ever since James's father had died.

The next guests to arrive were Tom and Janine Madison, newlyweds who'd bought a house four doors along from Elsa.

Right after Sam had been introduced to them, he heard the creak of a gate opening behind him. He turned, to see two women approach from the next-door yard....

A blonde and a redhead—the former wearing enormous elliptical tortoiseshell sunglasses; the latter carrying a tray of dinner rolls.

Sam recognized the redhead immediately as Deirdre Stafford, James's fiancée; and he noticed that though she must be in her mid-thirties now and had put on some weight since he'd last seen her, she was still, in an understated way, as pretty as she'd always been.

Her companion, however, was a *stunner,* leggy and slenderly built, with a confident sexy way of walking and eye-catching feminine curves in all the right places.

Vaguely, he was aware of James's satisfied, ''Ah, here's Dee!'' but his own attention was riveted on the other woman.

Her honey-blond hair was short. *Strikingly* short! Wavy and sun-streaked, it capped a beautifully shaped head. Her features were finely cut, her exquisitely shaped lips glossed with strawberry-red lipstick. She wore a scoop-necked black top, with a casual black skirt in some fluid fabric that swished around her ankles as she walked.

When he flicked his gaze back to her face, though he couldn't see her eyes he sensed she was looking at him...

And her exquisitely shaped upper lip was curled with disdain!

Startled, he raised his brows. What the heck had he done to warrant that?

But even as his mind boggled, she swiveled her shoulder to him and swept the basket of rolls from her companion.

"I'll take these inside, Dee." She sashayed away toward the kitchen door, and Sam found himself thinking she really had the cutest backside—

"Hang on!" James called after her. "Come and meet—"

"Back in a minute, James! Your ma will want to butter these rolls before putting them out." And then she was gone, the screen door flapping shut behind her.

James shook his head ruefully. "Like trying to catch a whirlwind. Meg's always been like that. You remember her, Sam? Dee's baby sister?"

Sam knew he was gawking. "Beanpole?" His tone was incredulous. "*That...was...Beanpole?*"

Dee chuckled. "Heavens, I'd forgotten that old nickname. Well, Meg did finally stop growing—"

"But not till she hit five nine," James said. "And she filled out," he added, straight-faced. "Some."

Some indeed! Sam thought, as he and Dee went through the obligatory "Hi, how *are* you!" routine. He hadn't seen Meg Stafford since she was thirteen or fourteen—she'd been a will-o'-the-wisp creature then, tall and skinny, always flying around with a bunch of friends, face always half hidden by a long untidy curtain of hair. Who'd have guessed she'd grow up to be such a beauty!

"Ma's going to ask you if you can put Sam up for a couple of days, Dee," James was saying. "Till the guest room renovations are done." James had bent over the barbecue and only Sam saw the look of dismay Dee turned on him. He saw her swallow; saw her hand go to her throat.

"Dee?" James looked round at her when he got no response. "It's not a problem, is it? Sam can have Andy's room—he's not coming back till—"

"Friday." Dee smiled at Sam. He thought the smile was strained. "We'd love to have you stay over."

"I don't want to impose," Sam said quietly. "I'll get a room at the Seashore Inn, I stayed there last time—"

"Forget it!" James waved the suggestion away. "Last time you were here, you were convalescing, you needed your own space. This time...hey, we want you close by."

Sam knew he hadn't imagined Dee's dismay; but he was at a loss to account for it. Before he could come up with even a wild guess as to its cause, Janine wandered over to talk to him and politeness decreed that he listen as she prattled on endlessly about some movie she'd seen the night before.

"Thanks for buttering the rolls, dear."

"Anything else I can do, Elsa?" Reluctant to go back outside, Meg looked hopefully around the kitchen.

"The wine's in the fridge. Could you serve it? You know where I keep the corkscrew. Use those glasses, dear." She indicated a tray of glasses on the countertop.

As Elsa bustled outside with the rolls, Meg took the wine from the fridge and noticed, as she filled the first glass, that her hand trembled.

No wonder, she thought bleakly.

Sam Grainger's expression of startled sexual awareness as he'd watched her walk through the gateway into Elsa's yard had thrown her for a loop. Thank heavens she'd been wearing her sunglasses, or he might have read her own equally jolting reaction to him.

When she'd confronted him on the beach earlier, she'd been so wound up she hadn't taken in too much of his appearance—though she'd certainly been aware of his cold green eyes and the hostile thinning of his lips. But coming over here to Elsa's, she'd been prepared for the meeting—or so she'd believed.

Still burning with resentment that he hadn't recognized her, she'd taken great pains dressing, needing the extra confidence that looking her best always gave her...but when she'd seen him gazing at her as if bedazzled, her heart had stuttered and almost fizzled to a standstill.

Catching her breath, she'd found her own gaze darting over him in flustered spurts—taking in his black eyebrows, his black-lashed eyes, his angular features, and the salon-cut black hair that sported its first threads of silver at the temples.

Sam Grainger had always been athletically fit, and arrestingly good-looking, but maturity had honed his muscled physique to a hard elegance, while the new lines fanning from his eyes and bracketing his mouth only served to enhance his appeal.

He was undeniably attractive.

And undeniably married.

He was also, Meg reminded herself starkly as she poured wine into the last empty glass, undeniably contemptible.

She put down the wine bottle and peeked out into the yard. She spotted him right away—even casually dressed in a cobalt-blue T-shirt and faded old jeans, he stood out in the crowd—as he would stand out in *any* crowd.

He was with Janine. The petite brunette was prattling, and giggling to beat the band. He was grinning down at her, his eyes crinkled, his sensual mouth slanted crookedly.

He was a heartbreaker. Tempting as sin itself...

Meg gripped the edge of the sink. An odd, jellying sensation quivered deep inside her as she faced up to the fact that this *devastatingly* attractive man was the father of her child.

Of course he knew nothing about it.

And wouldn't have cared, either, she reflected bitterly, even if he had. The morning after they'd had sex on the beach, he'd left Seashore at dawn in his spiffy scarlet Jag without bothering to contact her...and she'd never had so much as a postcard from him since.

Janine's giggle drifted across the yard and in through the open window...along with Sam's husky answering chuckle.

Meg's heart hardened to stone.

Angrily, she picked up the tray of glasses. What a *flirt* he was. Having the time of his life while his wife risked *her* life abroad.

If only Alix Grainger could see him now!

Sam rubbed a hand over his jaw as Janine moved away to join Elsa; his facial muscles ached from the effort of smiling at the girl's superficial chitchat. He glanced around to look for James...and saw Meg come out the back door.

She was carrying a tray of drinks—sparkling pink wine in green-stemmed glasses. He fixed his gaze on her, and perhaps his blatant appraisal distracted her because she stumbled. The glasses wobbled, clinked together, but as she regained her balance, they righted themselves.

Putting his beer can down, he made his way over to her.

"Hi, Meg, it's good to see you—"

The glasses tinkled again.

"Here," he offered, reaching for the tray. "Allow me."

"Thank you, I can manage." She tilted her chin haughtily and swung the tray away from him. "I'm used to waitressing, and I'm good at it. Now why don't you run along, Mr. Grainger, and do what *you*'re so good at!"

"And what would that be?" he asked, trying to sound faintly amused even as he felt a stab of surprise at her uppity attitude.

"Charming the ladies!"

She stalked away, leaving him blinking in astonishment. Her voice had positively dripped with sarcasm. What was *with* this female!

He took a deep breath, went to retrieve his beer, and drained the last of it in one long gulp. Women! Who understood them! Certainly not he. Never had; never would. Besides, he'd just legally disentangled himself from one; he was not about to entangle himself with another...no matter how attractive she was.

And he wasn't about to deny to himself that he found the new Meg Stafford attractive. *Physically* attractive.

But as to her personality...heck, when it came to that, he'd rather spend time with a disgruntled warthog.

"Honey," Dee whispered as Meg passed her a glass of wine from the tray, "I've something to tell you."

Meg scooped up the last glass for herself and bent briefly to set the tray on the grass, against the trunk of the apple tree behind her. She straightened and, poised to take a sip of her wine, looked questioningly at Dee.

"Meg, James has arranged for Sam Grainger to stay at our house for the next few days—"

"*What?*"

"Hush, don't screech—oh, everybody's staring!"

Meg spun her gaze from her sister—and as luck would have it, it clashed immediately with Sam Grainger's.

She whirled round, so her back was to him. "Say it's not so!" she hissed. "Dee, tell me you're lying. Joking. Whatever." She hauled her sister behind the tree. Swinging her glass to her lips, she drained it in three desperate gulps. "He can't come into our house!" She hiccuped. "It's out of the question. I don't want that man—"

"Are you, by any chance, talking about me?"

She gasped and whirled round. Sam Grainger's head was poked around the tree trunk. His eyes had a wicked glint. Incredible eyes, she couldn't help thinking even in her moment of distress; *alarmingly* hypnotic. The kind of eyes that could mesmerize a woman if—

"We...we don't have room for you, at—" hiccup "—our place. Sorry." She hiccuped again.

He chuckled.

Dee said, placatingly, "Don't be silly. Of course we do. Meg—well, she's just not used to wine. Not on an empty stomach. It went straight to her head."

"Well, good," Sam said. "As long as that's all it was, because the last thing I'd want to do is cause anyone any trouble. Thanks, Dee. And Meg—" deadpan "—I'm sorry about your...weakness. Maybe you should stick to lemonade."

And then he was gone, before she had a chance to make any of the snappy retorts she'd undoubtedly have managed to come up with had he hung around a moment longer.

"It's going to be all right." Dee gave her a consoling hug. "You just have to pretend you've never met him before but treat him politely. Can you do that, d'you think?"

"Sure!" Meg's snort was cynical. "Treat him like a

stranger. That's the trick, Dee. Why didn't I think of it myself?''

Because he's the father of your son, Dee could have said. But didn't.

''So…when is Alix coming?'' Dee asked Sam as the group relaxed over coffee, after a long and leisurely dinner.

Sam bit off an exasperated mutter. He'd hoped to get through the evening without anyone asking about Alix; but it was obviously not to be. ''She's out of the country at present,'' he said, avoiding a straight answer.

''I saw her on TV last night.'' Elsa shuddered. ''So brave, plunging into the middle of those awful wars, the way she does. She's a real heroine, in my humble opinion.''

Janine set her elbows on the table. ''Who's Alix?''

''Sam's wife,'' James said. ''She's a war reporter for a TV station.''

''Alix Grainger's your wife?'' Janine's eyes glowed as she looked at Sam. ''You must be so proud of her!''

''Alix is an…amazing woman.'' Sam spooned sugar into his coffee and stirred the coffee vigorously. When he looked up again, his expression was bland.

''And she's coming to the wedding?'' asked Tom.

''I'm sure she'll try to be here,'' James offered. ''It'll all depend on whether she can get home.''

''You live in Portland, don't you, Sam?'' prodded Angelina, the eldest of the Barnley sisters. ''In a luxury house, big enough for a family of six, according to James.''

''But you don't have any children, do you?'' said Monique, the middle sister, then frowned as the youngest, Emily, dug a warning finger into her ribs.

''It's not everybody that likes children,'' Emily said

soothingly. "Some men—well, they just want to have their wives all to themselves, not to share."

Sam was glad his hands were on his knees; this way no one would see that under the table, they'd clenched into hard fists. He loved kids; more than anything in the world he'd wanted to fill that house with children. He'd wanted to give them the kind of childhood he hadn't been fortunate enough to have himself; he'd wanted to have sons he could be proud of, he'd wanted daughters he could spoil rotten.

But because of Alix—because of her unforgivable betrayal—his hopes, his dreams, had all come to naught.

"Oh, I like kids," he said lightly. "But sometimes a couple can get caught up in the rat race and before you know it…" He shrugged.

Dee perhaps sensed his tension for she pushed herself up from the table, and put a steady hand on his shoulder.

"Sam, I'd like to get you settled in. Would you get your bag and I'll take you over to the house?"

"Sure, that'd be great—"

Meg lurched to her feet. "Give me a couple of minutes. I'll clear a few things out of Andy's room, get it ready."

Long shadows had fallen over the yard as the sun sank, and she had just a moment ago taken off her sunglasses. She looked straight at Sam as she walked by, and he felt as if a jolt of electricity had zapped him and stopped his heart.

Her eyes were huge, and blue as the sky. Good Lord, he thought, this was the oddball he'd met on the beach! But it wasn't that sudden startling realization that set his mind reeling, nor was it the blatant antipathy in her gaze.

What stunned him, and bewildered him, was something entirely different. It was the dread that emanated from her in waves—a dread so deep it shivered a chill down his spine.

Why was she so afraid of him? he wondered blankly, as he watched her walk away.

What had he ever done to her!

CHAPTER TWO

MEG raced up the stairs and into Andy's bedroom, her heart hammering with the erratic thuds of a pendulum gone berserk.

She swept a panicky gaze over Andy's picture wall, where he had painstakingly, over the years, hung every one of his sports pictures. Darn it, she thought with a feeling of desperation, why did the boy have to be such a jock!

She unhooked each photo where Andy was smilingly accepting an ice hockey award, a football medal, a baseball trophy. *Smilingly.* That was the operative word—it was the smile that might give him away. The more recent pictures, where he was scowling with typical preteen embarrassment, she left in place. She took down eight pictures in all.

She hurried with them to her bedroom, where she tucked them in the back of her closet, behind another much larger picture—one she'd hidden there five years ago after her divorce.

And as she saw it, inspiration struck.

Tugging the framed portrait from its corner, she blew dust from the glass, revealing Jack, Andy and herself. The picture had been taken at a Seattle studio when Andy was three. The photographer had remarked how much the boy resembled his father. Jack had glanced at her, but hadn't corrected the man. Andy had said nothing, either, because he'd been too young to know Jack wasn't his real father.

He and Jack hadn't *really* looked like each other—it

was just that they'd both had dark hair and blue eyes. It had been enough to fool the photographer...

And it would be enough, Meg prayed, to fool Sam Grainger.

With quick steps she returned to Andy's room with the family portrait and was about to hang it on one of the vacated hooks when she heard Dee's raised voice.

"Meg? Where are you?"

Her heart leaped. "In Andy's room," she shouted.

"You go on upstairs, Sam." The voice drifted up to her. "I'll follow with some clean towels."

Agitatedly, Meg hung the studio portrait, and after one last breathless scrutiny of the other pictures to check that she hadn't left one that might clue Sam in to the truth, she spun round and ran to the door.

In the doorway, she bumped into a solid body.

"Hey!" Sam's voice was startled. "Where's the fire?"

"Sorry! I—" She broke off with a protesting gasp as he dropped his travel bag and firmly clasping her upper arms, maneuvered her backward into the room. He smelled of the summer night and his own raw male musk.

She felt buried memories lurch to vibrant life.

She wriggled violently. He kept her imprisoned.

"Right." His eyes pinned her with laser-like intensity. "What gives?"

She swallowed. "What...do you mean...'what gives?'"

"Why the scream of horror when you found out I was going to be staying here?"

She opened her mouth to deny his accusation, then changed her mind when she saw his expression. Whatever lie she came up with, she knew he'd see through it. So...she didn't offer him one, just stared right back at him, defiantly, and snapped, "You're the lawyer. Why don't *you* figure it out!'' She finally managed to wrench herself free. She stumbled back.

He stepped forward—

Dee sailed in. ''Sam, I've brought your towels. Has Meg shown you the bathroom?''

Meg seized the opportunity to flee. ''Will you show him around, Dee? I have some things to do in the kitchen.''

She took off before Dee could say anything, brushing past their unwanted guest without another glance.

Damn Sam Grainger! she reflected hotly as she stormed down the stairs and along to the kitchen. He hadn't been back in Seashore for six hours and already he was turning her life upside down.

Again.

Treat him as if he were a stranger, Dee had advised.

But how could she, when just being close to him had unearthed hidden memories in her heart. Memories of that night. Under the tree, on the beach below the Seashore Inn.

The night Sam had heard, on the TV news, that his wife Alix had been killed in a helicopter explosion, in a tragic accident over the Mediterranean.

The night that had changed Meg's life forever.

She'd just turned eighteen and had recently graduated from high school, with plans to go to college in the fall. She'd taken a summer job waitressing at the Seashore Inn, and had started work the very day Sam Grainger had checked in for a week's vacation.

''Doctor's orders,'' Deborah Wilson, the assistant manager, had confided in Meg. ''He's been really ill with some vicious virus—on the mend now, but he's been told to have a week on the coast, get some bracing sea air.''

Meg hadn't seen Sam since she was fourteen. Though

he'd worked summers at the inn during his early student years, and had later often spent part of the Christmas holidays at the Carradines's with James, he'd never come back to Seashore after he and Alix Merrick had married.

Word was Alix hated small towns; word was Sam doted on his wife and her slightest wish became his desire. Meg had thought it terribly romantic...but she'd missed his visits.

And she was pleased he'd come back; however, he didn't come into the dining room that night, and the head waiter told her he'd had his meal sent up to his room.

She was disappointed. But if he was here for a week, he'd surely come into the dining room at some point, and they could renew their acquaintance. Not that he'd ever paid her much attention in the past—he was ten years older; she'd been just a kid—but when their paths had crossed he'd always treated her in a friendly teasing way and she'd liked him. Liked him a lot. In fact, she'd idolized him the way she might have admired a favorite movie star: he was *incredibly* good-looking but so very far beyond her reach she didn't waste even one single moment dreaming about him!

That night she was going off duty at eleven, was trundling her bike along the side of the inn, glad it was a lovely moonlit night for the ride home, when she noticed a tall figure standing alone by the water's edge.

The beach was deserted.

The figure was Sam.

After only a moment's hesitation, she dumped her bike, and made her way down the still-warm sand to join him. The tide was coming in, the waves whispering their mystic secrets. The smell of salt was in the air, and the scent of dried seaweed from crispy fronds tossed up by the last tide.

"Sam?" she said tentatively as she came up behind him.

He spun round, and in the pale light from the sky she saw that his cheeks were wet. And his eyes were haunted.

"Sam...what—"

"Who is it?" he asked harshly. "What the hell do you want, following me down here at a time like this? Can't you see I want to be alone?"

"It's me...Beanpole. Sam, what's happened?"

He was wearing only jeans; no shirt, nothing on his feet. She saw his bare chest rise and fall sharply. "You haven't heard?"

"Heard what?"

He delved trembling hands through his hair. "The news. It was on the ten o'clock news. I was watching it in my room." His voice cracked. "Alix. She's been killed...abroad..."

"Oh, Sam—" She'd closed the space between them as he hunched over and started to sob. Great dry wrenching sobs. She wanted to put her arms around him but was too inhibited. Instead, she wrapped them around herself and murmured useless words of comfort while her heart ached in sympathy. "I'm sorry. So sorry—"

As the memories surged, Meg's eyes blurred. Sam had been devastated. Totally devastated. It was as if the very bottom had dropped out of his world. She'd never seen anyone so broken.

After a while, they'd walked, back up the beach, and along to the ancient arbutus tree, where the beach ended and the grass and wildflowers and forest began. And there they sat, in the moonlight, Meg whispering words of comfort while Sam spilled out his agony and his grief.

Looking back afterward, she'd never been able to pinpoint the exact moment when the comfort had become physical. Had it been when she put her arms around him as he started to shake? Or had it been when he put his arms around her when she began to sob. Or perhaps it had been—

But no point in asking herself that now. She'd never know the answer. All she knew was that at some point she'd been running her hands up and down his bare back and murmuring words of compassion while his tear-damp face was buried against her shoulder, his fingers tangled in her long hair. And then he had uttered a despairing groan, his hot cheek was against her own...and then his lips were against her lips, his hands were on her breasts, and his mouth had taken hers in a kiss that rocked her to her foundation.

From then, it was hot and desperate and totally out of control. She couldn't have stopped him...or herself...even if she'd wanted to. Which she hadn't...

Afterward, when she'd gotten up, and started putting on her clothes, he'd walked—naked and with the stiff steps of a robot—down to the water and straight into the ocean.

Her heart had almost stopped. Was he going to...?

She waited, pulses thudding, as he swam and swam and swam.

And not until she saw him swim ashore again, saw him stride out of the water in the moonlight like some god from the sea, did she breathe a shuddering sigh of relief.

She wanted to go to him, desperately wanted to go to him...but she guessed he'd need to be alone...

And she needed to get home. Dee would be wondering where on earth she was.

She slipped away up the grassy slope, clambering, her body aching, her legs trembling, her head spinning...her cheeks and lips soaked with salty tears.

When she finally reached the place where she had left her bike, she drew in a ragged breath and looked back...

To the place where she had left her virginity.

She could see Sam standing there now, a lonely solitary figure. With his back to her, he was gazing out over the moon-silvered waters. As if the encounter between them had never happened.

She felt a sliver of pain pierce her heart.

Just as if it had never happened.

"It's going to be all right, Meg." Dee came quietly into the kitchen. "Sam says he won't be hanging around here much—he plans on doing a lot of hiking, and sailing."

Meg turned from the window, where she'd been staring out but seeing nothing. "What's he doing now?"

"He's in the bathroom, getting washed. He's going to bed—said he's tired after the drive, needs an early night."

Meg slumped with relief. "Good. Maybe by tomorrow, I'll have gotten a grip—"

"The worst's over. That first meeting."

"But he still has to meet Andy," Meg said. "Dee, I'm not going to breathe easily till the wedding's over and he's gone back to Portland—"

"He asked who Andy was. He could see it was a boy's room, but he said he'd assumed, when we mentioned Andy, that he was an adult—a boarder."

"What did you say?"

Dee shrugged. "Just that he was your son."

"He didn't…pursue the matter?"

"I could see he was taken aback. I told him Andy was at camp—and then I excused myself quickly before he could ask any questions and said I'd see him in the morning."

"I took down all the pictures of Andy, the ones where he was smiling—"

"I didn't notice—"

"Excuse me, ladies!"

Meg jerked her head round as Sam's voice cut into their conversation. She hadn't heard him out in the corridor, hadn't heard him push the door open. He was standing in the doorway, in his T-shirt and jeans, the hair at his temples damp, as if he'd just washed his face. Tensely she wondered if her words had been audible to him as he approached. She thought, by his open, casual expression, that they had not.

"Yes?" Her tone was sharp.

"I just wanted to say good-night and to thank you for letting me use your son's room."

"You can thank him yourself when he comes home," she managed to say coolly.

"He looks like a fine boy. Sporty type?"

"Yes."

"My kind of guy." He leaned a shoulder against the doorjamb and looked interestedly around the kitchen. "It must be sixteen years since I was in this room but it still feels familiar to me. You've modernized it, of course— I have a vague memory of olive-green appliances and green and orange wallpaper!—but you've managed to keep the cozy ambience it had in your mother's day..."

"Dee told me you were bushed," Meg said crisply. "Don't let us keep you up. You've had a long day."

"Meg!" Dee sounded shocked.

"It's OK, Dee," Sam drawled. "Beanpole was never known for her tact." He yawned. "But she's right. It's time I turned in—oh, could I have a door key? I may go out early, wouldn't want to leave you asleep with the doors unlocked."

"Meg, don't you have an extra key in your purse?"

Meg scooped her bag from the table and as she took out the key, Sam walked over. He was so close she smelled his minty toothpaste. His jaw was darkly shadowed; she sensed that if she were to touch it, it would be sandpaper rough. It had been sandpaper rough that night, she remembered; next morning, her skin had been grazed, grazed and tender...

She swallowed, tilted back, and held out the key.

"Thanks." His fingertips caressed her palm as he took the key. Accidentally or otherwise, she didn't know.

Didn't want to know!

She snatched her hand back, and clutched her elbows.

"This for the back, or front?" he asked.

"It's the same key for both locks," Meg said shortly. "Good night."

"Good night. And good night to you. Dee. It's great to be back in Seashore...and I really appreciate your putting me up."

"It's good to see you again," Dee said. "Sleep well."

Sam sketched a brief salute, and shoving the key in his hip pocket, strolled from the kitchen.

Neither Dee nor Meg spoke till they heard, through the ceiling, the click of his bedroom door closing.

"You were very rude," Dee said.

"Not half as rude as he was to me thirteen years ago!" she retorted caustically.

"Upstairs...when I brought the towels...the air was fraught with tension. Had you been talking—about that night?"

"No, he didn't so much as hint at it! And until he does he'll hear no mention of it from me—I wouldn't demean myself to bring it up! He's acting as if it never happened, just as he did way back then. And doesn't that tell you what kind of a man Sam Grainger is?"

"I really don't understand him, Meg. James and he have always been such friends...and you know how decent and ethical James is! I can't imagine him holding Sam in the esteem he does if Sam didn't deserve it."

"James doesn't know about that night. James doesn't know—" Meg lowered her voice to a hissed whisper "—James doesn't know that Sam had sex with me and never bothered to contact me afterward in case I'd gotten pregnant. If James knew that, if he knew Sam was Andy's father, he might pretty fast change his opinion of his oh-so-perfect best man!''

"I really trust James's judgment of people, honey. Maybe Sam had a very good reason not to contact you.''

"Like *what*?''

"I don't know!'' Dee shrugged helplessly. "We've had this conversation a hundred times, haven't we? We've asked ourselves that question over and over and over. And we've never yet come up with a satisfactory answer.''

"That's because there isn't one!'' Meg said. "The man just has no sense of responsibility. Or *accountability*.'' She sighed. "I'd wish I'd never met him if it weren't for Andy. I do owe him for that. I can't even begin to imagine what life would be like without—''

She broke off abruptly as something occurred to her. A cold clammy sensation slid down her spine. "Oh, Dee—'' her voice quivered with dismay "—what if Sam finds out the truth and tries to take Andy away from me! A boy his age does *need* a father, I *know* that! But I couldn't bear it if he chose to live with Sam and Alix—''

"Meg, for heaven's sake, stop worrying about things that are not going to happen. There's no way Sam's ever going to find out the truth. You and I are the only two in the world who know it, and he's certainly not going to hear it from me!''

"Nor from me!'' Meg breathed out, her eyes shut. "He'll certainly never hear it from me!''

Sam woke very early to the sound of the steadily pounding surf and the strident hyow-hyow of an angry gull.

For a moment he didn't know where he was, but when he turned his head and saw the picture wall it quickly came back to him.

He was in the Stafford house. In Meg's son's bedroom.

Andy. Sam grinned. Super-jock!

Shoving back a swathe of tumbled hair, he got up. Ambling to the window, he flicked open the venetian blind—and blinked as the sun dazzled his eyes.

The water was aglitter with silver sequins, the sand stretched out like a curved ribbon of cream silk, and the beach was deserted but for a distant figure to the south.

He'd go for his morning run, he decided; by the time he came back the household would in all likelihood be stirring, and then he could shower without wakening Dee or her sister.

He tugged on his jogging shorts, went through his stretching routine, put on his running shoes, and slipped quietly from the house via the back door.

He jogged down the beach till he reached damp sand.

After a brief hesitation he started running south, in the direction of the Seashore Inn.

He breathed deeply of the tangy air as he settled into a steady rhythm. This was the life, he reflected. The air was as clear as crystal, as intoxicating as champagne.

He'd fallen in love with Seashore the very first time he'd come here. And he'd envied James, because James had been born and brought up in the quiet little town.

"But I'll have to leave Seashore for good, once I graduate," James had said matter-of-factly. "I'd never make a living here as a lawyer, not in a tiny place like this."

So James had eventually joined a law firm in Seattle, while he himself had settled in Portland, where he'd been born and brought up.

But Seashore had remained, in a private corner of Sam's mind, as a vision of paradise. An impossible paradise; one that was out of his reach...

Legs pumping like pistons, breathing coming more

heavily, he saw that he was halfway to the inn and he let his gaze roam over it.

The sprawling three-story building sat high above the beach, as pretty as a page from a picture book with its slate roof, heritage-blue siding, white gingerbread trim, and white-painted verandas. Blue and white curtains billowed at open veranda doors; blue and white umbrellas shaded the patio tables below; and a recently clipped lawn sloped down to the beach, dew glistening its smooth emerald surface.

He squinted. Something was on the lawn—a sign of some kind. He couldn't read it from here, he was too far away.

Curiosity piqued, he stepped up his pace.

Meg leaned weakly against the red-barked trunk of the arbutus tree, still trying to catch her breath.

This morning she'd run harder than usual, wanting to be out of the house and home again and showered before Sam Grainger made an appearance. But she'd overdone it, and by the time she'd reached her usual turning spot—this madrona tree just below the inn—she'd felt dizzy to the point of seeing stars, and had flopped down in the shade of the tree.

When she'd finally felt better, and was about to drag herself to her feet, she had then—and only then—spotted a wooden sign on the inn's lawn, a sign that hadn't been there the day before. She'd gazed at it curiously, and when she read what it said, she'd gaped at it, eyes stuck wide open for minutes on end, before she collapsed against the tree trunk again, wilted as a dead flower.

The sign was large; the words black-painted on white with the name of Seashore's one Realtor, and his phone number, scrolled stylishly below them.

FOR SALE
Burton Barton
Seashore Real Estate—

Meg still gawked, her mind still disbelieving what her
eyes were seeing. How she'd missed the sign on the way
here, she hadn't a clue—

No, that was a lie. She knew only too well. She'd
been so wrapped up in her own problems, she'd been so
worried about Sam Grainger being in her home and
about his inevitable upcoming meeting with Andy, that
she'd been blind to her surroundings as she jogged.

But there it was.

In all its glory.

The Seashore Inn, where she'd worked for most of the
past thirteen years, was up for grabs.

Anxiety cramped her stomach and questions blud-
geoned her mind. Why hadn't Mark told her he was
planning to sell? Who would buy the inn? And most
importantly of all, what would the changeover mean, in
terms of her own job security?

Mark, in his position as owner/manager, had only last
week promoted her to assistant manager, the promotion
to take effect at the end of September when Deborah
Wilson, his present assistant, was due to retire. Meg had
been thrilled with the challenge of the extra responsibility—and had been delighted at the prospect of a higher
salary.

But now...that might change. She reminded herself
that sometimes new owners had their own agendas—and
sometimes they brought in their own people for key po-
sitions...

She blew out a weary sigh and riffled her fingers
through her damp feathered hair—and became aware, for
the first time, of heavy footsteps pounding toward her.

With a quick frown she glanced round. And only
barely managed to stifle a resentful mutter when she rec-

ognized the person intruding on her solitude. Scowling, she scrambled to her feet.

Like her own, Sam Grainger's hair was damp, and sweat ran down his chest, playing peek-a-boo in the silky black curls. He was wearing only jogging shorts and runners. She recognized the designer labels on both... and the sour thought came to her that she could have fed Andy for three months on what his father had spent on his running outfit.

"Hi." He hovered a few yards away. "Going back now?"

Tersely, she nodded.

"Hop to it, then!"

He turned without waiting for a response, and loped off at an easy pace.

Hop to it? Her scowl became a dark glower as she watched him go. She wasn't about to hop to his, or any other man's command! Besides, she couldn't think of a more unpleasant way to start the day than running alongside Sam Grainger!

But she couldn't hang around here all morning...

She set off, deliberately holding back, and fell into her own regular pace several yards behind him.

A mistake.

From the front, he'd been awesome.

From behind, he was utterly breathtaking...

That jet-black hair, those wide shoulders, that muscled back, that lean waist, that oh-so-delectable—

She swiveled her gaze to the ocean, refusing to gawk at him. But she immediately got dizzy with her head twisted to the side. She locked her jaw and stared front again. Immediately the willful and wayward twin that lived inside her shoved the prim and proper twin aside; and wild and wayward took up where it had left off before prim and proper had so rudely interrupted.

—Butt, and those magnificent thighs, and—

He'd picked up speed. Muscles rippled, legs pumped powerfully, strong arms swung rhythmically.

Prim and proper rolled its eyes, and gave up a losing battle. This time around, it was no contest!

Meg groaned.

It was truly awful, sometimes, being a Gemini!

Sam glanced back over his shoulder as he heard a groan, and only barely managed to suppress a loud guffaw.

Jogging was supposed to be good for relieving stress; it apparently wasn't doing the trick in Meg's case! Her features were contorted in a grim scowl—and her sky-blue eyes, as they'd clashed with his questioning gaze, had positively sparked with animosity.

He'd managed to suppress the guffaw. He didn't manage to suppress a grin. She was something else, Meg Stafford—

But she wasn't Stafford anymore, was she! That gold-framed picture on Andy's wall—that was a family picture. But where was Andy's father now? There'd been no sign of male occupancy in the bathroom, but the man could be at camp with his son, or perhaps out of town on business...

Sam slowed his pace, waited for Meg to catch up.

When she did, he opened his mouth to speak but she went speeding right past him. Arrogantly. Head held high.

Her quick steps left imprints on the damp sand. Like a trail. Inviting him to follow.

Picking up his own speed again, he chased after her, but the lady was fast! He didn't catch up with her till they were on the final stretch.

Panting lightly, he jogged alongside her with easy strides. And felt a sense of unadulterated male satisfaction when he saw that her face was dripping with sweat, her breathing rasping and labored.

"Hey," he said. "Slow down. I want to ask you about Andy's father—"

Not a good move.

She twitched like a startled filly—he only caught a fleeting glimpse of the shock and dismay in her eyes—and then veering away from him, she shot off. Making not for home, but for the water.

She paused before the foaming wavelets only long enough to rip off her runners, and then—in her perky white shorts and her snugly fitting candy-striped tank top—she plunged headlong into the surf.

CHAPTER THREE

SAM had just completed his cool-down routine when Meg headed back to dry land.

He watched, hands planted lazily on his hips, as she splashed out of the water and stomped toward her runners.

She looked fit to be tied. Was she angry because he'd hung around? He chuckled; she'd be even more incensed if she could see herself! Her flight into the ocean had been impulsive; she hadn't given herself time to think of how she'd look when she came out. Her sopping tank top clung to her breasts, and her saturated shorts sucked against her lower torso like a second skin—a transparent second skin. He swallowed hard to choke back laughter as he saw that under the shorts she was wearing a pair of shocking pink bikini briefs with a sprinkled pattern of black spiders.

She glared at him, then turning her back, she stuck her feet into her runners. Crouching, she fastened the laces.

She really had the cutest rear end—

She swooped up again and around. His gaze, of its own accord, flicked back to her breasts. Lust stirred...

Nostrils aflare, she abruptly tugged the wet tank top clear of her flesh...and held it out there. Water dripped from her hair, from the tip of her nose, from her chin...

"What are you waiting for?" she asked, her tone icy.

"An answer to my question...about Andy's father."

"I'm divorced." She flipped her head brusquely and cool droplets arced from her hair across his chest. "Not that it's any business of yours. Jack and I got married, our marriage was a mistake, and we parted.'' She spun away from him and started up the beach. Fast. ''Amicably.''

He followed, lengthening his stride in an effort to catch up. ''Where is he now?'' he called after her. ''Jack?''

''He moved away, after the divorce. We've lost touch.''

''Isn't that hard on Andy?''

She stopped and whirled round, so abruptly that he'd bumped into her before he could stop, and knocked her off balance. He swooped forward and grabbed her just before she hit the sand backward.

He swung her upright in a fluid tangoesque sweep, and held her tight. He heard her breath coming fast, felt the goose bumps on her flesh, smelled the salt tang in her hair.

She tried to wriggle free, but he didn't release her.

''Isn't that hard on his son?'' he repeated.

Her eyes were flinty, but her lips were trembling. Was that from the cold water...or because the lady wasn't as in control as she'd like him to think? Did she still feel the wounds of a broken marriage? He knew how that could hurt. He felt a surge of compassion.

''Meg—''

''What's hard,'' she snapped, ''are your fingers digging into my arms!'' She wrenched herself free. ''Look, I've gone along with having you in our house, because it's a favor to James and Elsa. But don't push your luck. If you persist in poking that long Grainger nose into affairs that are none of your business, you'll be out on your ear faster than you can say 'homeless'! Do I make myself clear?''

He opened his mouth to say ''Crystal!'' but she'd already gone. Up the beach she ran, across the road, over her lawn, and around the side of her house with the speed of a gazelle fleeing from a raging forest fire.

Thoughtfully, he stood there, his mind awhirl with questions—questions he'd better not ask, he decided dryly, or he'd end up on the street.

But he'd sure as hell like to know what it was about him that riled her so much!

Meg stared aghast at her reflection in the bathroom mirror. No wonder the man had been ogling her with the glazed eyes of a toddler gazing at a chocolate sundae. She presented an erotic image straight out of a girlie magazine.

Shivering, she skimmed her appalled gaze over herself, from the apple-round outline of her breasts so blatantly revealed under the clinging cotton of her saturated top, to the spider-patterned bikini pants so clearly exposed through the wet shorts plastered like cellophane to her flesh.

Oh, she had never felt so *mortified.*

Whirling from the mirror, she turned on the shower till it was as hot as she could bear it and blindly she stepped under the stinging spray.

But as her chilled body started to thaw out, she forced herself to think objectively about Sam Grainger. And about his blatant sexual interest in her—which was inappropriate, to say the least, considering he was married. She also forced herself to acknowledge her body's involuntary sexual response to his interest—a response which existed no matter how she might try to fool herself it didn't.

Her lips tightened as she vigorously shampooed her hair. When Sam Grainger saw her, did he think about that night on the beach? Did he remember the passion that had erupted like flame between them? Did he recall her mindless arching up to him when he caressed her breasts? Did he recall her wanton moans, her whimpers, her wordless cries of delight as he set her body on fire? Did he remember how those sounds had further fueled his own desire till he'd groaned aloud as he brushed kisses over her heated flesh, to every intimate part of her?

What had happened between them that night had been, to her, a stunning revelation. She'd never experienced such ecstasy; such a soaring of joy. It had been like leaving earth and moving into another dimension. The memory had been buried deep inside her. but had never been forgotten.

In Sam Grainger's case, it had been dismissed as if it had never happened.

She must remind herself of that, when he gazed at her with that flare of desire in his eyes. He might want her again, as he had before, but she would never again give in to him. Even if he wasn't married, she'd feel exactly the same way.

It was confusing, though, terribly confusing. How could she possibly still feel so so drawn, physically, to a man whose character she absolutely *abhorred*!

Sam followed Meg's path around to the back door, and when he went into the kitchen he found Dee at the stove. His mouth watered as he was met with the aroma of frying bacon mingled with the tantalizing smell of brewing coffee.

The screen door creaked shut behind him, and hearing it over the crackle and spit from the frying pan, Dee turned from her task, spatula in hand. Her shoulder-length auburn hair was still damp from her shower, and she looked fresh and pretty in a blue blouse and a summer skirt. She greeted him with a quirked eyebrow and a meaningful glance at the wet track that ran from the back door to the corridor.

"Let me guess," she said. "You and Meg had an argument and you dumped her in the sea?"

"No, the swim was her own idea. And no, we didn't have an argument—" He paused, and hearing the steady hum of running water that assured him Meg was in the shower, he went on quietly, "She's changed, Dee. I don't remember your little sister being so...touchy. She told me she was divorced and heck, all I did was ask her wasn't it hard for her son, not seeing his father, and she blew her—"

The spatula slipped from Dee's hand and clattered to the tiled floor.

"Oh, darn..." She stooped to retrieve it and when she straightened, her face was flushed. "Sorry." She discarded the spatula, opened a drawer and took out another. She returned her attention to the frying bacon and with her back to him, said in a muffled voice, "You were saying?"

Was he imagining the tension in the air? No, he could feel it quivering between them, just as tension had jerked between Meg and him when he'd asked about her husband. Feeling as if he were walking in the dark without a flashlight, he said, in an offhand tone, "Oh, nothing much. I guess Meg doesn't like talking about her ex. Can't blame her—divorce is never pleasant, no matter how amicable the separation. Now if you'll excuse me, I'll go upstairs and have my shower when Meg gets finished in the bathroom."

He was almost at the door when Dee said, "Sam?"

He stopped, turned. "Mmm?"

Her expression was strained. "Jack wasn't cut out to be a dad. He never did have much time for Andy, so when the marriage broke up..." She bit her lip.

"You're saying, he was no great loss. At least as far as his son was concerned."

"After the divorce, both Meg and Andy put Jack behind them. Neither of them talks about him, so it would be better if, while you're here, you avoid the subject.''

''I surely will. And Dee...thanks for setting me straight.''

As he made his way upstairs, Sam cursed himself for having ever asked Meg about things he had no business asking about. Dammit, why had he opened his big mouth? He'd not only upset Meg, he'd upset Dee, too.

He passed the bathroom. The door was closed, but the shower was no longer running. He could hear the high-pitched whine of a blow-dryer.

He went into his bedroom—and stopped short when his eyes lit on the family portrait of Jack, Meg and Andy.

He walked slowly across the room and stared at it.

If what Dee said was true, and after the divorce Meg and Andy had put Jack behind them...why had they never taken this portrait down and put it away?

It just didn't make sense.

He was still staring at the picture, trying to come up with an answer, when he heard a sound behind him. He glanced round.

Meg was standing in the corridor, her tall leggy figure wrapped in a faded ankle-length pink robe, her hair pet-alling her head in a dazzle of white-gold.

''I just came to tell you,'' she said, ''that I'm finished in the bathroom.''

Her gaze slid past him, to the portrait. When she looked at him again, her eyes had a panicky look, as if she expected him to throw more questions at her.

Instead, he just said, ''Thanks.''

He saw a shadow of relief cross her face. But she said nothing more, just nodded her head and walked away.

''What made you come here a few days early?'' Dee asked Sam.

Because it was such a lovely sunny morning, Dee had

set breakfast out on the patio. Meg never ate breakfast, and while Dee and Sam had tucked into bacon, eggs, and sausages, she had poured her usual mug of black coffee. And while Dee and Sam had chatted casually about this and that, she had—rudely—buried herself in the morning newspaper.

She had to suffer Sam Grainger's presence in the house; there was nothing to say she had to enjoy it.

And she was determined not to!

"I'd just finished a particularly vicious divorce case," Sam was saying. "Two little kids were involved and the parents were using them as pawns. I thought I'd gotten pretty hardened over the years, but something about this case just got to me. I needed a break."

"Well, you've come to the right place. I'm going to miss this peaceful little town when I move to Seattle with James." Dee chuckled. "I sometimes have to pinch myself to make sure this is all really happening—heavens, James and I have known each other all our lives, but only as friends, and it was quite a shock, to both of us, when we realized our friendship had grown into something else."

"Certainly not a case of love at first sight!" Sam teased.

"No, not like you and Alix!" Dee returned. "Now there was a marriage made in heaven. Did you ever hear how Sam and Alix met, Meg?"

Meg gritted her teeth. She counted to ten, then dropping the paper a little, she looked over top of it at her sister. "Sorry." She managed a vague, not-really-interested tone. "Did you say something, Dee?"

"I was just asking...did you ever hear the story of how Sam and Alix first met?"

"No." Meg folded the newspaper carefully. "I didn't." She glanced at her watch and with a "Look at the time!" lurched to her feet. "My goodness, I'm going to be late. If you'll both excuse me, I have to leave now for work.''

Dee's face was scarlet with embarrassment. Meg felt a stab of remorse. She really was being unbearably ill-mannered. No matter how callously Sam had treated her in the past, it wasn't fair to take her resentment out on him in a way that put Dee in an awkward position—

She forced herself to look at Sam.

''Tonight over dinner,'' she said in as friendly a tone as she could drum up, ''you'll have to tell me how you and Alix met. I'll look forward to hearing it.'' She bent and dropped a kiss on Dee's cheek. ''Bye for now.''

After Meg left, there was silence for a little. And then Sam said, ''Where does Meg work?''

''At the Seashore Inn. She's head receptionist.''

''Has she been there long?''

He saw Dee's eyes widen, as if his question had taken her by surprise—he couldn't think why.

''Meg started as a waitress in the dining room, just after she graduated from high school.'' Dee suddenly busied herself refilling their coffee mugs. ''Her very first day...well, it was the same day you arrived here thirteen years ago, when you came to Seashore to convalesce...''

Sam had no recollection of seeing Meg at the inn. All his memories of his one and only stay there as a guest were tied up with the devastating grief that had consumed him when he'd heard the TV report that Alix had been killed.

A report that had turned out to be false. Oh, the helicopter had exploded all right, but Alix had not been on it. It had been about to leave the airfield when she'd been taken violently ill with stomach pains. She'd been rushed by ambulance to the nearest hospital, where she'd had her appendix removed in short order.

But he hadn't discovered that till early next morning.

And the hours between the report of his wife's death and the discovery that she was alive were lost to him forever; lost in a mental blackout caused by a mixture of the vodka he'd consumed to numb his pain, and the powerful medication he'd been taking for the damned virus responsible for his having to take convalescent leave in the first place—

"Ah, you're up and about!" James's voice greeted them from the open gate between the two properties.

Sam shook his head to clear it of the old memories, and watched his friend stroll over and give Dec a warm kiss.

"So—" James took Meg's vacated chair "—what are the plans for today?"

"You and I have to go see the church organist," Dee said. "Then we have an appointment with the minister at eleven, and after lunch we're driving Elsa to Larch Grove to shop for her new shoes. Sam—" She turned to him with an apologetic smile. "Can you entertain yourself today?"

"Hey, no problem."

Actually, he couldn't wait to be alone.

And when James and Dee did finally leave, he heaved a sigh of relief. They had no idea he was feeling so low, so restless, so...empty. Nor did he want them to know. But a week here, with no worries, no deadlines, should do him a world of good.

But even as he tried to convince himself, the prospect of returning to Portland after the wedding and going back to the work he hated brought him out in a cold sweat.

"Ah, *there* you are!" Meg muttered. "Finally!"

With half an eye on the inn's owner as he entered the foyer, she finished watering the potted begonia plant on her file cabinet and tucked the water jug under the reception desk. Then setting her fists on the counter, she gave him her full attention as he strolled over to the desk.

"Good morning, Mark." Her tone was mildly aggrieved.

"And the top o' the morning to you, Marguerite." He flashed her a wide white smile. "How are you, after your day off?"

Mark O'Driscoll, a still-handsome man in his early seventies, was the only person in the world who called her by her given name. When he'd interviewed her thirteen years ago for the waitressing job, he'd addressed her by the name typed on her résumé—and she hadn't thought it politic to tell him she preferred "Meg." By the time she'd felt comfortable enough to do so, some weeks after she'd been working there, it was too late. No matter how often she corrected him, he never called her anything but Marguerite.

And when she'd chanced to find out that his beloved wife, who had died just after their thirtieth anniversary, had also been called Marguerite, her heart had melted. And she'd never again asked him to call her Meg.

But at this moment, her heart wasn't melting. Far from it! Over the years, he'd become a good friend, both to her *and* Dee, but good friends didn't keep secrets like this from each other.

"How am I? Well, I was just fine, until I saw that For Sale sign today! What the heck's going on? You've always sworn that when you left the Seashore Inn for good, it would be feet first! You don't look to me as if you're dead, Mark—in fact..." She narrowed her gaze as she scanned his smoothly brushed salt-and-pepper hair, his new-looking yellow shirt and smart yellow and white checked slacks. "I've never seen you look so *jaunty*!"

"Jaunty?" He chuckled, and his eyes sparkled. "Is that right, mavourneen?"

He looked as if he had a happy secret he was barely managing to keep. Meg felt her heart soften. "OK," she said, a smile in her voice. "Out with it."

He came closer, so close she could smell the lemony aftershave he slapped on every morning. "Marguerite, I'm getting wed again."

Meg gaped at him. Speechless.

He laughed at her surprise. "To Deborah."

Deborah? The assistant manager who was due to retire next month? "But…you and Deborah have never got on! You've done nothing but fight ever since I've known the pair of you! Bicker, bicker, bicker…"

"Aye." Mark's face sobered. "It wasn't till I knew she was leaving that I realized—well, just how much I'd miss her. And it wasn't as if she was going to be staying on here in Seashore. She's planning to spend her retirement traveling the world. It's been her dream. And when I told her, the other day, how much I'd miss her, she snapped back, 'Well, why don't you just come along for the ride!' And before you could say Fodor's Travel, I asked if she was proposing marriage and she said, well, she certainly wasn't proposing to spend her golden years living in sin!"

"Oh, Mark…" Tears in her eyes, Meg leaned forward and gave Mark a hug. "I'm so happy for both of you."

When she drew back, he said, "The contract you and I signed, after you accepted the new position—"

"It becomes invalid once the inn changes hands?"

"Aye, it does. But I'll give the new owner a glowing report, Marguerite. Whoever takes over here, I'll make sure he knows you're the best person for the job. Bar none.''

"Thanks, Mark. But that's not your worry now. You and Deborah must concentrate on yourselves, enjoy your retirement. You've both worked hard and deserve it.''

After Mark left, Meg felt her shoulders slump.

And felt a stab of envy for Mark's obvious happiness.

What was wrong with her, she wondered, that she had never found the right man? Was the fault in her? Was she too difficult to please? What was she waiting for…a knight on a white charger? She muttered a self-derisive "Humph!" If there had been any romance in her soul, Sam Grainger had knocked it out thirteen years ago; and Jack had given it another kick a few years later!

Her attitude to life was now one of harsh realism; she no longer believed in romantic love. When she looked at men, she saw them only too clearly, with all their warts. And she didn't mean only the surface flaws; she dug deeper, and didn't blind herself to the character flaws.

Sam Grainger was a prime example of that.

She could see how a romantically inclined woman could easily tumble head over heels in love with the man. He was not only drop-dead gorgeous, he had charisma and presence and warmth. Superficial warmth, however. Underneath, he was cold. Careless. Irresponsible—

"Good morning." Mrs. Morgan from Room 215 smiled at her from the other side of her desk. "My husband and I should like to order a picnic basket. Vegetarian, please."

"Certainly, Mrs. Morgan," Meg said. "I'll arrange that immediately."

And as she turned her attention to the job, she managed to push her personal problems to the side. But even there, they continued to niggle at her all day; and when she went off duty at five, they were still niggling at her.

As she cycled home along the beach road, she found herself hoping that Sam Grainger wasn't around. And when she reached Seaside Lane and saw that his Infiniti was not in the driveway, she felt a surge of relief.

Relief that intensified when Dee told her Sam had left a note saying he'd gone out and wouldn't be back till late.

"Poor man, he feels in the way," Dee added gently.

Meg grimaced. "My fault. I did mean to be pleasant, though, over dinner. Or at least polite. But I have something else to worry about besides Sam Grainger. Dee, you'll never guess what's happened—I tried to call you but you've been out all day!" She took a glossy brochure from her bag and thrust it at her sister. "The inn's for sale!"

Dee scanned the real estate brochure briefly before dropping it on the table. "Yes, I know. James and I had coffee this morning in the Hava-Java and we noticed the ad in Burton's window next door. Why's Mark selling, Meg?"

Meg threw herself down on a chair and detailed her conversation with the inn's owner. Dee, who liked Deborah as much as she liked Mark, was as delighted as Meg that the the two were to be married. But shadowing that delight was the anxiety over Meg's future at the inn.

"The timing's awful!" Dee's mouth drooped at the edges. "What with the house payments and all."

Meg ran a hand over her nape, felt it slick with sweat. Their widowed mother had left the family home to them jointly on her death fifteen years ago, but just last week Dee had announced that she was gifting her share of the house to her sister, and from the day of the wedding

Meg would be sole owner. Meg had been astounded by her sister's generosity, but thrilled with the arrangement.

"You'll have to come up with the mortgage payments yourself," Dee had warned. "We won't be sharing expenses any longer. But with your new job, it'll be well within your reach. And James and I—well, we can't afford to be paying mortgages on two houses, so it'll work out well for all of us!"

It had seemed like a wonderful arrangement. At the time. Now it felt to Meg like a burden, and one that might sink her. But she didn't want Dee to worry.

"Don't fret, Dee. I'll manage. If worse comes to worst, I can always do like Elsa and take in boarders." She tried to sound cheerful, but the thought of taking in boarders sent a faint shudder through her. She couldn't bear the idea of having strangers living here...

After she and Dee ate dinner, she went for a long walk alone by the ocean. It should have helped her pounding headache, but it didn't. When she got home she took a couple of aspirin and went to bed.

But she was still wide awake hours later, when she heard Sam Grainger's black car glide up the drive.

Sam let himself in quietly by the back door.

Flicking on the light, he yawned. He'd spent the day hiking along the coast, then he'd enjoyed a seafood plate at the Seashore Pub, after which he'd had a couple of pints while he chatted with some of the locals.

He yawned again. The sea air was soporific. He'd sleep like a log tonight, no doubt about it.

As he crossed the kitchen, he noticed a glossy brochure lying on the table—and he recognized the Seashore Inn on the front. Meg must have brought the flier home from work.

He scooped it up, and a printed leaflet fell out. It was

the MLS info for the property. It was all there—from the square footage to the number of rooms to the price.

He whistled.

Pretty steep.

He slid the leaflet back into the brochure and replaced it where he'd found it.

But ten minutes later, as he lay in bed and was just dropping off to sleep, the image of the glossy brochure surfaced in his mind. The picture of the attractive inn…and the printed detail of the not-quite-so-attractive price.

He could swing that price, of course.

He and Alix had already sold their luxurious house in Portland, and had divided up all their assets. He'd insisted she keep the London flat he'd bought her ten years ago—her base when she was in Europe. Because she herself was now a top earner, she hadn't wanted alimony, but had instead requested a one-time lump sum— a huge sum but one he could afford. Just as he could afford to buy the inn…if he sold his shares in the firm—

You're Grainger, Grainger and Grainger now, son. His father's harsh voice echoed from the past. *Your grandfather's gone, I'll soon be gone. The firm's in your hands, your hands alone. Guard it. Pass it on to your own sons. This is your family heritage, your responsibility…*

The night breeze gusted in through the open window, snaking a chill over Sam's naked body. He shuddered. Was his father trying to exert his will from the grave? Was he still trying to control him, as he'd done till the day he died a year ago?

Sam felt a twist of pain as memories flooded his mind. Nothing he had ever accomplished had been good enough to satisfy Fergus Grainger. Hell, as a dutiful son he'd even gone to law school when his father had demanded it; and had joined the family firm...when the last thing he'd wanted to be was a lawyer, *especially* a divorce lawyer. But all his efforts to gain Fergus Grainger's approval had been in vain. The kind of father-son relationship Sam had yearned for as a child and hoped for as an adult had never materialized.

He lay on his back, wide awake now, and stared up at the shadowy ceiling. His father was gone. He was his own man...at last...

But he wasn't *seriously* thinking, was he, of giving up his law career and buying the Seashore Inn?

CHAPTER FOUR

MEG was out on the back lawn early next morning, going through her regular pre-jog stretching routine, when she heard someone open the kitchen door behind her.

Bent over, fingers dipping to the ground, she darted a glance round and saw Sam. He was wearing shorts and runners. As he walked over to her, her pulse gave a panicky flutter. Those legs of his were so long, so powerful...so close.

"Going for your run?" he asked.

His jaw was dark-stubbled and his hair fell aslant his brow, giving him a rakish look that tugged at something deep inside her. She wrenched her gaze from him and threw him an aloof "Shortly", while continuing with her routine.

He started jogging, circling her. She sensed he was watching her. Avidly. Probably goggling like a teenager at the glimpse of creamy flesh revealed under the hem of her skimpy purple satin shorts with each downward lunge.

She gritted her teeth and, seguing into the next segment of her routine, said with a derisive curl of her lip, "Don't you *stretch* before you run?"

"Already have," he said. "Upstairs." And added, with barely suppressed laughter in his voice, "Naked."

No way did *that* deserve a response. But she couldn't control the blush that burned her cheeks. Sending a volley of hostile vibes his way, she stretched, and stretched again—all the time acutely aware of his amused gaze on her.

By the time she was through with her complete rou-

tine, perspiration was trickling down between her
breasts, and she knew it hadn't been caused by the heat
of the sun.

Ignoring him, she swiveled away and made for the
street. He caught up with her and together they jogged
down to the beach. Once there, Meg took off northward.

"Hey!" Sam was obviously taken aback. "Where are
you going?"

"This way. To Matlock's Marina."

Her heart thudded four times before she heard him
call after her, "I'm going along to the inn. See you
later."

She kept running.

And was disconcerted by her let-down feeling. Good
grief, she hadn't wanted to spend time with the man, had
she? No, she certainly had not! But she had to admit—
despite her intense aversion to him—that she felt more
alive when he was around. More…aware.

Well, he really was *fantastically* good-looking. Any
normal female would surely need some kind of psycho-
therapy if a magnificent male like Sam Grainger left her
cold.

Physically, that was.

She snuck a furtive glance over her shoulder, but he
was pounding south toward the inn…

And, she noted with an uninvited and unwelcome feeling of chagrin, *he* wasn't sneaking any peeks back at
her!

As Sam approached the inn, he wondered if he was
crazy, to be considering what he was considering: giving
up a profession where he'd achieved not only outstand-
ing financial rewards but much-valued respect from his
peers.

It was difficult to contemplate change, to contemplate
a future where he would manage his life, rather than

life—in the guise of his father—controlling him, as had been the case for the past almost-forty years.

He slowed his pace, and let his eyes scrutinize the imposing blue and white property in a much different way than he had yesterday, when he'd just regarded it with casual interest and a lingering affection from the past.

Now, in his heart, he felt a rush of exhilaration—something he hadn't experienced in years. Yes, he decided; he was going to look into buying the Seashore Inn.

And he wasn't going to let the salt grass grow under his feet! As soon as the Realtor's office was open, he'd drive along there and talk to Burton Barton.

Meg got back to the house before Sam.

When she came out of the bathroom after her shower, she heard him in his bedroom and she called "Bathroom's empty!" Then while he was showering, she quickly dressed, and hurried downstairs.

Grabbing a mug of coffee, she said to Dee, who was turning a batch of hash browns in the frypan, "I'm going to drink this on the run. I want to get in early—Theresa's taking over for me in reception because I'll be in Deborah's office most of the day, working my way through a mile-high pile of paperwork that needs to get done before the changeover. It's going to be hectic for the next while."

"I wonder who'll buy the place?" Dee asked absently.

"It'll be an out-of-towner," Meg declared as she went out the door. "Nobody around here has that kind of money!"

Burton Barton was a hearty type with a ginger mustache and an energetic mass of graying ginger hair. Florid-faced and overweight, he dabbed his brow frequently with a caramel-brown bandanna as he ushered Sam into his private office.

"The Seashore Inn won't be on the market long." He lowered himself heavily into his big chair. "Places like that are hard to come by around here…and the inn is a jewel. It needs refurbishing—the owner has let it slide a bit over the past dozen years—but basically the property is sound. Have you been inside, had a look at it?"

"Not recently, but I'm familiar with it." Sam sat back, propped one jean-clad leg over the other at the knee. "I worked there for a few summers in my early student years, filled in wherever I was needed…the bar, the dining room, the kitchens, the gardens. Got a good feel for the place."

"So you know Mark?"

"Oh, yeah."

Burton glanced at the business card Sam had given him. "You're a lawyer." When he looked up, his eyes were curious. "You're planning to give all that up?"

"Time for a change," Sam said.

Burton raised his bushy eyebrows. "Quite a leap!"

Yes, it was quite a leap. What Sam didn't tell the Realtor was that as a student he'd taken to hotel work like a frog to a pond; from the first day, he'd felt at home in the Seashore Inn, had felt he'd truly found his milieu. In fact he'd told his father, after his second summer there, that he wanted to go into the hotel business, but Fergus Grainger had flown into such a towering rage Sam had felt not only his body but his soul shrink. So much so that he'd never raised the subject again. Even now, remembering that painful scene, he felt the same chill he'd felt then.

He realized Burton was waiting for a response.

"Yeah," he said casually. "It's a leap, but in the direction I want to go."

The door opened and the secretary brought in coffee and cookies. After she'd gone, for the next hour or so he and Burton discussed the hotel, and Burton answered all of Sam's questions. But when the Realtor finally heaved his massive body from his chair and said he'd take Sam over to the inn, show him around, Sam shook his head.

"I want to play this low-key." He got to his feet. "Right now, I'd appreciate if you'd keep my interest in the place confidential, till such time as I make up my mind whether to move on it or not. I'll drop by the inn today, have lunch there, make my interest known to Mark, and just wander around the place. Then either way, I'll be in touch with you again."

But as Sam walked out to his car, he knew he'd already made up his mind. He wanted the inn. Wanted it more than he'd ever wanted anything. But he reined in the hot urgency pounding through his veins. He had to keep a cool head, had to make sure he didn't let emotion blind him.

The asking price was steep; he had to assess what the inn was worth, to him, before he made his offer.

At the inn, he met with Mark and they had a private talk over a long lunch. Then for the next few hours he prowled unobtrusively in and around the building, giving it a thorough inspection... and in the process, reinforcing his desire to become the inn's new owner—subject, of course, to having it first checked out by a building inspector.

Later, after mulling over what he was willing to pay for the property, he drove to the Realtor's office. There he had Burton write up a conditional offer, which he then signed before returning to the Stafford house.

He found Dee alone, Meg having called earlier to say she'd be working late. He and Dee had dinner together, and afterward, while she spent the evening writing thank-you letters for wedding presents received, he did some chores for her, including fixing a leak under the bathroom sink.

He was in the kitchen around ten-thirty, enjoying a solitary mug of cocoa and thinking about going to bed, when he heard steps outside on the path.

He found himself smiling in anticipation of provoking Meg's stubborn scowl...but when he put down his mug and opened the door he found Elsa on the stoop.

She walked in, a red Pyrex casserole in her hands.

"Hi, Sam. Your room's ready. I was wondering why you hadn't turned up till I discovered James forgot to pass on the message this afternoon." She indicated the casserole. "My fridge is packed and I want to ask Dee if I can store this here—it's for the rehearsal dinner tomorrow night."

"She's gone to bed, Elsa. With all the last-minute preparations for the wedding, she said she was beginning to feel like a spinning top that had gone out of control! But I'll take that." He put the dish in the fridge.

Elsa glanced around. "Where's Meg?"

"Still at the inn."

"What's she doing there at this time of night?"

"Overtime, I gather."

"Odd. I've never known her to work evenings before."

Sam gave a lopsided grin. "Then maybe she's just avoiding me."

"Why would she be avoiding you?"

"She doesn't like me and hasn't bothered to hide it!"

Elsa snorted. "Likes you too much, in my humble opinion. Heck, Meg Stafford had a crush on you from the first time she set eyes on you!"

Sam laughed. "You're wrong there, Elsa. Besides, the

first time Beanpole set eyes on me she was only ten or eleven, didn't even know the opposite sex existed!''

"You don't know much about little girls, Sam Grainger!'' Elsa's eyes glinted. "No, it's my humble opinion that Meg's still got a soft spot for you and since you're a married man she's not wanting to get too close to the flame.''

"Flame?''

"When a man and a woman spark off each other the way you two did at our barbecue the other night, there's going to be a flame. Meg's a nice girl, Sam. She's not into hanging around with somebody else's husband—heck, she knows the trouble that can cause. Hasn't she already gone through the pain of having a sly young thing steal her own!''

"I got the impression the divorce was amicable—''

"And pigs can fly—ohmigosh, I almost forgot! I have biscuits in the oven! Look, come over when you're ready. Come to the back door, I'll be in the kitchen.''

After she'd gone, Sam made his way upstairs. The house was quiet; the only sound the beat of the surf drifting through the open window of his room.

So, he reflected as he stripped his bed, the divorce hadn't been amicable. Meg's husband had—apparently—left her for another woman. The old old story. But not the story *Meg* had told him. And could he blame her? He wasn't about to tell anyone the wretched details of what caused his own marriage breakup.

It didn't take him long to pack his bag, and once he'd zipped it up, he slung it over his shoulder, put off the light, and made his way downstairs.

Meg was almost home when she saw the light go out in Sam Grainger's room. She breathed a sigh of relief.

He'd gone to bed.

Thank goodness.

She yawned. It had been a long day. But Mark, who normally didn't encourage his staff to work overtime, had been grateful that she'd offered to stay and keep working her way through the paperwork that had to be done before the changeover.

He'd indicated to her that the Realtor already had three prospective buyers lined up. But though he'd assured her again that he'd do everything in his power to make sure she wouldn't lose her promised promotion, she still couldn't help worrying about it.

She hopped off her bike and wheeled it over the lawn to the back door. Propping it against the wall, she opened the screen door quietly, unlocked the back door, and slipped into the shadowy kitchen.

She clicked on the light.

And shot her hand to her throat when she saw the tall figure coming into the room. So...their unwelcome guest was still up after all. "Oh, hi!" Her voice shook a little. "I thought you'd gone to bed!"

"Relax," he drawled. "I'm just leaving."

Only then did she notice the travel bag looped over his shoulder. "Leaving?"

"My room's ready next door." His mouth curved in an amused smile. "You won't have Sam Grainger to kick around anymore!"

That smile. So like Andy's it threatened to turn her heart to mush...if she let it, which she had no intention of doing. "Where's Dee?" she asked.

"Gone to bed. She was exhausted."

She opened the door again. "Don't let me keep you."

"So...see you tomorrow night."

"Tomorrow night?"

"The wedding rehearsal. At the church."

"Oh. Right." How could she have forgotten about that? What was it about this man that rattled her so that her thoughts wouldn't stay in order?

He hitched his bag higher on his shoulder and sauntered across the kitchen. He paused as he came alongside her and stood so close she smelled chocolate on his breath.

"Just one more thing," he murmured.

Her breath caught in her throat. What did he want? His eyes had gotten so dark; as if the thoughts behind them were dark, too. Dark with...desire? She swallowed. Flexed her knee, ready to use it if she had to.

He slid a hand into the hip pocket of his jeans and came up with the house key. "There you go." He dropped it into the breast pocket of her shell-pink blouse without letting his fingertips make any contact with her flesh.

Why, then, did her breasts swell? Was it possible that they had retained a memory of that night, that night when she and Sam had—

"What's up?" he asked lazily. "All of a sudden, you look a million miles away!"

No, just three miles away, she could have said; under the madrona tree below the inn. But would he want her to remind him of that night? She thought not!

But she couldn't help wondering if, after their passionate moonlit encounter, he'd been plagued by guilt. As she had been, for the *longest* while. She'd tortured herself mercilessly, wondering if what she'd done had been a sin: she'd had sex with a married man. But of course she hadn't known at the time that he was still married. Nor had Sam. They had both truly believed his wife was—

"Meg?"

Sam's voice rasped into her thoughts and as she refocused her gaze, he waved a hand before her eyes.

"The lights are on," he said lazily, "but is there anyone home?"

She blinked. "Sorry. I was...dreaming..."

Night scents wafted through the open doorway. The smell of sun-dried grass, roses, and seaweed. It was a night for walking on the beach, hand-in-hand with a lover.

A dangerous image.

She banished it, and replaced it with the safer image of his vibrantly beautiful wife.

"Alix," she said. "When are you expecting her?"

She sensed a snap of tension in him. Or had she just imagined it? Must have, because when he spoke, it was in a casual tone.

"With Alix, I never know. She just...turns up." He yawned. "Well, I'm bushed. I'm going to call it a night." He made to turn but paused. "Oh, by the way, when did you say your son was due back?"

The question was so unexpected she didn't have time to brace herself. As her legs threatened to buckle, she grasped the edge of the door more tightly. "Tomorrow. Late evening. Why?"

"He looks like a neat guy. I'd like to get to know him." He turned, and this time he really did go.

Meg tried to speak, but her throat had tightened as fear rushed through her. She didn't get the words out till after he'd disappeared into the dark, through the low picket gate adjoining the two properties.

"But...you'll be leaving here the day after the wedding," she called after him. "Won't you?"

The only answer she got was the slap of Elsa's door shutting. Sam had gone inside. He hadn't even heard her question.

Slowly, Meg closed and locked her own door. Leaning back against it, she stared blindly into space.

Sam liked the look of Andy. Liked the look of his own son. Thought he was a neat guy.

Meg bit her lip so hard she winced.

Not for the first time she wondered if she'd been

wrong, thirteen years ago, in deciding not to tell Sam she was expecting his child. She had kept her secret for what she sincerely believed were all the right reasons; but if he ever discovered the truth about Andy, would he be able to see it that way? Or would he be absolutely furious and condemn her out of hand for not telling him something he'd undoubtedly feel he had every right to know?

She prayed she would never have to find out!

Next morning, after helping Elsa with the breakfast dishes, Sam drove to the Realtor's office, eager to hear what the response had been to his purchase offer.

"Mark has come back with this counteroffer." Burton gave the papers to Sam then mopped his brow with an orange bandanna as he eyed his client across his desk. "You have till midnight to make up your mind."

Sam twisted his mouth as he read the typed figure. "He's driving a hard bargain. But...I'm going to try to screw him down another notch."

"You've noticed he's thrown in the adjoining property. Five acres of brush..."

"Yeah, that's a real sweetener. OK, I'll up my offer and meet him halfway." Those five acres of brush had particularly caught Sam's eye when he'd hiked over it the previous afternoon. It would be perfect for chalets. "And we'll make this counteroffer valid till 10:00 a.m. tomorrow."

Sam waited in Burton's office till the secretary had prepared his counteroffer, then he read it and signed it.

As Burton walked him across the outer office, the Realtor said, "As you asked, Mark and I have kept the negotiations confidential. And by the way, he's delighted your offer was better than those of the other interested parties."

"Terrific." Sam stepped out into the street. Somebody

had finger-scrawled McKenzie's Carwash on the dusty body of his Infiniti. Grinning, he turned to Burton, who had lumbered out in his wake. "Am I crazy, to want to live in this sleepy little town?" His tone was wry. "Sometimes it feels to me like stepping into the past."

"Nothing wrong with stepping into the past, Mr. Grainger." Burton raised his orange bandanna in salute to an elderly woman walking their way. "Good morning, Elvira."

"Get about your business, Burton Barton," she snapped back as she sailed by. "You'll not make any money standing out on the sidewalk. Your father would turn in his grave!"

"People." Burton's florid cheeks balled as he beamed after her military-erect figure. "That's what Seashore's all about, Mr. Grainger. People!"

Sam was driving back along Main Street when he caught sight of Meg trudging along the sidewalk, heavily weighed down by bulging plastic grocery bags with the red SureBuy logo.

He slowed the car, pulled up alongside her. She turned her head and he saw that her eyes had a strained expression.

"Hop in," he said. "I'll drive you home."

She flushed. "Will you *please* stop following me?"

"*Following* you?"

"Even at the inn!" There was no mistaking the accusation in her tone. "I wasn't going to say anything—but don't think I didn't hear you were hanging around out there yesterday for the best part of the—"

"So now I'm a stalker!"

"Your word, not mine!"

"I assure you, Meg, I have not been following you." This *was* the most infuriating woman he had ever met! "Now, do you want a drive or not?"

She hesitated for a moment, then said, ungraciously, "Only because I'm behind schedule—no, don't bother to get out, I can manage." She snatched the back door open and loaded the bags onto the seat. By the time she slipped into the front beside him, she was breathless. Within seconds her subtle peachy scent had perfumed the car's interior and he felt a rush of pleasure as he inhaled it.

Her skin was as sweet, he reflected wryly, as her mood was sour!

"Not at work today?" He pulled out into the street.

"I took the day off. With the wedding tomorrow, there's a whole bunch of last-minute things to do. I've promised Elsa to make four different kinds of salad for the rehearsal dinner tonight."

"When do you go back to work?"

"Monday."

"Who looks after your son when you're at the inn?"

She had been slouching back in her seat; now from the corner of his eye, he saw her straighten her spine.

"I've been very fortunate," she informed him, "that Dee works from home, and Elsa's usually around, too. But my son is twelve and he's perfectly able to look after himself."

"You and Dee and Elsa..." Almost to himself, Sam mused aloud. "Andy's close to three women...but no father figure around. I guess he sees James, but only once in a while..."

"What are you implying?"

Startled by the harshness of her tone, he jerked his head round to look at her, and was taken aback by the glitter of anger in her eyes. Where did this anger come from? His statement had been casually uttered, without the slightest nuance of criticism in his voice.

"Didn't mean to offend." He set his jaw grimly.

He turned onto Seaside Lane and said no more. But

he could feel the hostility emanating from the woman beside him, and he was determined, this time around, to get to the bottom of it.

He pulled into the Carradines's driveway, and erupting from the vehicle, he strode around to the other side. Meg had already gotten out and was opening the car's back door.

Firmly but without force, he set her aside.

"I'll get these." He dragged out the bags and levered the door shut with his hip. "Lead the way."

Animosity quivered from her stiffly held figure as she marched over the lawn, up the neighboring drive, and around the side of her house to the patio. She flicked out the screen door, opened the back door and turned.

"Thank you, I'll take those now—"

He strode past her and dumped the bags on the table.

He heard a thumping sound upstairs. Dee. Good. She was out of the way. He didn't want her to hear this.

He moved to block Meg's escape route to the hallway. Setting his fists on his hips, he glared at her.

"I want you to tell me," he said, "why you can't stand the sight of me!"

Her face had grown pale. "Please leave."

He shook his head.

"If you won't, I will." She made to sidestep him.

He grasped her by the shoulders.

She tried to twist away.

He looped his arms around her waist, held her in an inescapable position. Her breathing was ragged, her eyes wild.

She had never looked more beautiful.

And clamped close to him, the way she was, she had never seemed more desirable.

Oh, blast! He didn't want to want her! All he'd wanted was to find out why she disliked him so intensely. But with that tousled blond hair smelling like peaches and her skin looking like fresh cream, his need to know was melting into a need to press his lips to hers and discover their taste and their texture. The thought aroused him. And he knew, by the widening of her eyes and the darkening of their color, that she had become aware of his desire.

Her body trembled. Her eyes half closed. And he knew, without a doubt, that she wanted him, too. He hissed in a sharp breath, and sliding his hands down her hips, cupped her curvy bottom, pulled her closer—

The outraged gasp from the doorway behind him took a second to register. When it did, his first thought was, Dammit, Dee, where's your sense of timing!

His second thought was, That didn't sound like Dee!

Even as those thoughts darted through him, Meg was wrenching herself free.

He heard her say, in a horrified tone, "Oh!"

With a sheepish smile on his face, he turned, ready to placate Dee with a light apology.

Only…the person facing them from the open doorway wasn't Dee. It was a good-looking lad of around twelve or thirteen. Tall. Dark-haired. Blue-eyed. Finely cut features set in a black glower.

Stafford features.

Meg's features.

As Sam ran a swift gaze over the lean figure in the gray T-shirt, baggy khaki shorts and rumpled gray socks, he noticed the boy was clutching a framed picture—but for the moment seemed to have forgotten it. His attention was focused solely on his mother.

"Andy!" Meg ran a hand shakily through her hair. "When did you get back? I wasn't expecting you till—"

"Yeah." The boy's voice was scornful. "That's obvious!" He indicated Sam with a sneering jerk of his head. "So, who's the boyfriend?"

"*Andrew!*" Meg took a step toward him, but stopped

short when he swept up the picture he was clutching and held it between them like a wall. Sam saw that it was the family portrait from the boy's picture wall.

"What's *this* doing in my bedroom!" The boy crashed the framed portrait down on the table with such force it was a miracle the glass didn't shatter. "What's going on, Mom? I'd really like an explanation!"

CHAPTER FIVE

MEG stared at the picture, dismay swirling through her. But when her gaze jerked back to Andy and she saw that his anger was about to boil over again, she felt a rush of panic.

The words "Damage control!" shrilled in her brain, and hoping she didn't look as shattered as she felt, she acted on them.

"Sam," she said quickly, "I want to talk to Andy…alone. Would you leave us, please?"

He frowned, obviously balking, and she guessed he was loath to desert her. She hardened her gaze, and waited.

After a tense pause, he nodded. "Sure, whatever you want."

But as he passed by her, on his way out, he said in a low voice, "I'll be next door if you should need me."

"Thanks, I can handle it."

She waited till the door had closed behind him before taking in a deep breath and turning to Andy with a smile.

"Well," she said, "how about a hug? I've missed you!"

He didn't move.

She crossed to him, gave him a quick hug.

"Who is he?" Glaring at her, Andy pulled away and stood rigidly. "Where did you pick him up?"

She ignored the blatant insult, sensing that his anger was rooted in insecurity. What he needed from her at this moment was warm reassurance, not harsh censure. "He's James's best man. He's been sleeping over here

71

because Elsa didn't have his room ready for him till last night.''

"Sleeping where?'' His jaw had a belligerent jut. "With *you*?''

She suppressed her irritation. "He used your room.''

"That jerk was in my room?''

"Elsa asked Dee if we'd put him up. Dee could hardly refuse, considering how good Elsa has always been to this family.''

"How come he was *groping* you?''

"He wasn't groping me.'' Yes, he *had* been groping her! She could still feel the jolt her heart had given when he'd cupped her bottom and hauled her against his hard body! "Heavens, Andy, the man's married. We... actually, we were fighting and I tried to take off and he grabbed me to stop me. I dislike him and he wanted to know why.''

"Oh.'' Andy thought for a moment, and then squared his shoulders. "In that case... well, he'd better watch out. I don't like him, either, and if he bothers you again, I'll—''

"What, Andy?'' Her smile was dry. "He's bigger and stronger than you.''

"Yeah, maybe, but I'll make sure I get in a couple of blows where it hurts, before he takes me.'' He shifted his glance to the picture on the table. "So... what about *that?*''

"He was showing too much interest in... our situation so I hung the picture up before he moved in, to forestall any further questions about... your father.''

"And you took down some of the other pictures to make room. I'll put them back now.''

"Oh, I shouldn't bother,'' she said quickly. "You're going to be moving into Dee's room soon, so let's leave hanging the pictures till then, OK?''

"Yeah,'' he said. "OK.'' He paused, and then said

gruffly, "I thought, when I saw that picture on my wall—and when I heard a man's voice down here—I thought maybe Jack had broken up with his bimbo and you'd let him come back."

"You know I'd *never* do that!"

"I guess not...but you had me worried for a minute. I shoulda known, though, that would never happen."

"No, that will never happen."

"So...who is this guy?" he asked, still grudgingly.

"He used to come to Seashore years ago—he worked at the inn as a student—and sometimes spent Christmas with the Carradines. He and James were at university together. He hasn't been to Seashore for years, though." Meg cleared her throat. "His wife doesn't care for small towns. You may have seen her on TV. Alix Grainger."

"Alix Grainger? Really? Yeah, I've seen her." He shifted awkwardly on his feet. "Mom?"

"Mmm?"

He flushed. "I...bought something for you." Digging a hand into the deep pocket of his shorts he came up with a small box. "Here." He held it out.

"What is it?"

"Well, open it and you'll find out!" His tone was edged with childish anticipation.

In the box was a heart-shaped dendritic agate, set in silver and hung on a silver chain. "Oh, Andy, it's lovely!"

"You really like it?"

"I adore it." She slipped it on, fastened the catch. "There, how does it look?"

"Yeah." His eyes sparkled with pleasure. "Looks really good on you." Grimacing, he gave her a sheepish hug. His breath smelled faintly of garlic; his black silky hair smelled of wood smoke from a campfire. "I'm glad I'm home."

"I'm glad you're home, too," she said softly.

"So." He turned and scooped up the picture. Dangling it from his fingertips as if it were a piece of foul garbage, he said, "Where do you want *this*?"

"At the *very* back of my bedroom closet."

"Gotcha!"

As he started toward the door, she added, "You haven't told me why you're home early."

"Mr. Gardner had to come back—family emergency—and so three of us guys had to accompany him, or there would have been too many left for the cars leaving later on."

"Did you have a good time?"

"Yeah, it was OK."

And that was all, Meg knew, that she would get out of him about that. At least for the moment. Oh, she'd hear every detail over the next few days, but it would come in dribs and drabs, when *Andy* felt like talking about it.

Thank goodness he hadn't felt like talking any more about the family picture. Thank goodness he hadn't used the incident to latch onto the topic of who his father was.

She knew, of course, that one day she'd have to tell Andy the truth. After the divorce, he'd brought the subject up from time to time but she'd always managed to ease him away from it. Recently, though, he'd taken to plaguing her about it and it was getting much harder to fob him off.

Last time he'd brought it up had been the week before he left for camp. "It's my *right* to know!" he'd cried. "Mom, every kid should know who his *father* is!"

The tearful yearning in his eyes had torn at her heart.

"Andy, I can't tell you. Not yet, at any rate. It wouldn't be fair to him—"

"Why *not*?"

She'd hesitated...and then decided to bite the bullet. "Because your father's married."

He'd gasped, shocked.

"Andy—" she'd put up a hand to halt the questions tumbling from him "—I'm sorry. I *will* tell you one day, I promise, when you're older..."

"Was he married when you had sex?"

Ouch! A blunt question and one to which she couldn't give him a straight answer. It would be too dangerous, too risky, to say, "He *was* married...but we both thought at the time that he wasn't." If that story got around...well, many people in Seashore were aware that for a period of about seven hours Sam Grainger had believed his wife to be dead.

"Andy, your father's a man you can be proud of. He's highly successful in his field and very popular."

Andy had scowled. "Does he...have any other kids?"

"Not as far as I know...but then, I haven't seen him since—" she'd swallowed over the lump in her throat "—since the night you were conceived."

"So he used you and then took off. He sounds like a jerk to me, Mom." Contempt hardened his eyes. "A total jerk! We're both better off without him!"

Yes, Meg had thought the same thing for years.

And in the few days since Sam had come back into her life, he had given her absolutely no reason to change her opinion of him. It would be a relief when he was gone and she could once again relegate him to the back of her mind.

But there were things to be got through before then. And the first of those was the wedding rehearsal tonight.

Sam glanced at Meg as he walked her back down the aisle for the umpteenth time as the rehearsal finally ta-pered to an end. From the moment she'd arrived at the church, she'd treated him with an aloof politeness that was like a wall of glass between them. So far, he'd been unable to break through it. But he wasn't done trying!

"So," he said, raising his voice over the organ's exultant swell, "did you sort things out with your son?"

"Yes." She kept her gaze fixed ahead. And added, regally, "Thank you."

The interior of the church was hot, and the warmth had intensified the peachy perfume she wore, mingling it with the essence of her own feminine scent. The intoxicating mix danced though his blood like silver bubbles of champagne. Distracting. Disturbing. "Andy's not in the wedding party?"

"No."

"I thought he might have been an usher." On leaving the chancel, he'd tucked her arm through his, despite her hissed protest. Now, as she tried to tug her fingers free, he swept her hand onto his forearm, imprisoning it there with his own. He was wearing a sports shirt and he felt the resentful thud-thud-thud of the pulse at her wrist, as it beat wildly against his hair-roughened skin.

"He didn't want to be."

"And did you want to be maid of honor?"

"I did," she said with a disdainful toss of her head, "until James announced you were to be his best man."

He chuckled softly. He sure got a kick out of needling her. Got a kick, too, out of looking at her! She was pretty as a buttercup this evening in a yellow top and miniskirt, with her hair as bright as sunshine, its cropped style revealing the sweet curve of her cheek.

Fantastic cheekbones.

Fantastic...everything!

He tilted his head back as he walked and let his gaze sweep down over her curvy bottom, neatly encased in knife-sharp pleats; and further down, following the slender lines of her endlessly long legs to the low-heeled yellow sandals.

When he looked back at her face, he could see the grim set of her luscious pink lips and knew she'd been well aware of his intimate scrutiny.

"I hope," she snapped, "that you'll manage to keep your eyes facing forward tomorrow as we walk out of here."

"I hope so, too!" They came to a halt as they reached the narthex. She yanked her hand free, and he grinned down at her, enjoying the flush on her cheeks that made them rosy pink as her lips. "But I'm afraid we can't count on it!"

Her flush deepened, but before she could respond, the minister began issuing some final instructions to the wedding party, prior to telling them they could all leave.

While he was talking, Meg had stolen the opportunity to sidle away from Sam. And the moment the minister dismissed them, Sam noticed her slip quietly around the edge of the lingering group and make for the front door.

With long purposeful strides he followed her outside.

The church was on a maple-lined street, and as he left the confines of the modern wooden building, the breeze gusted a few dry leaves along the sidewalk. The air smelled of sea salt and summer, garnished with the tantalizing aroma of fried onions from Harry's Hamburger Joint across the way…and the faintest peachy scent lingering in Meg's wake.

She was running down the flight of steps leading to the sidewalk. He took the steps three at a time and caught her up as she reached the sidewalk.

"How did you get here?" he asked. "Bike?"

She kept going. "My bike had a flat—I didn't notice till I was ready to leave. James was driving Dee but they'd gone by then, so I walked. And please don't offer me a drive back. It's a lovely evening for walking."

He kept his face straight. "My sentiments entirely," he said. "Which is why I left my car at Elsa's."

He deduced from the exasperated heavenward rolling of her eyes that this news did not make her day.

"I guess you were in such a hurry," he teased, as he strode alongside her, "that you didn't notice it in the driveway."

"I noticed it," she retorted. "I just assumed you'd gone in James's car."

"Ah, so you did think about me!"

"No, I did not *think* about you. It was just a passing...observation."

She picked up speed, the zigzag hem of her miniskirt kicking up with every step. He had no problem keeping up with her...though it *would* have been fun to walk behind! Those long fabulous legs—

"So," she said, flashing him a sky-blue look, "when's Alix arriving?"

"She's not coming."

"You've heard from her?"

"I haven't."

"I guess she'd have phoned if she'd been coming?"

He grunted something noncommittal. So far he had told no lies, unless you counted lies of omission. With a bit of luck, he'd get through the wedding without having to disclose the news of his divorce. The last thing he wanted to do was cast a blight on James and Dee's wedding day—

Oh, who did he think he was kidding! The reason he'd never told anyone he and Alix had split up a year ago, nor divulged to anyone that their divorce had just become final this week, was that he didn't want to see the expression in people's eyes when they found out that he...a divorce lawyer...couldn't even keep his own marriage intact.

Loss of face, that's what it was all about.

And he knew Alix wouldn't be rushing to spread the news, either: once the media got hold of the story, they'd poke and pry and might discover why her husband had divorced her. It would reflect badly on her—on her *image*...

And to Alix, image was all.

"You never did tell me," Meg said in a careless tone, "how you and Alix met. Dee implied it was a big deal."

Safer ground. "Alix hired me as her lawyer when she wanted to divorce her first husband. We fell in love. Love at first sight, as Dee mentioned."

"The thunderbolt."

He gave a light laugh. "Right. The thunderbolt."

"I didn't know Alix had been married before."

"One of those teenage disasters. Hormone-driven. They had nothing in common...other than that they both grew up in the same little hick town. Alix was career-oriented from the word go and couldn't wait to get out into the world and make her mark; Jeff Merrick was a down-home type of guy—his roots were in Hicksville, too deep for him to dig up. Even if he'd tried to, which he didn't. They got married because they wanted each other. In bed. Lust, not love."

They walked on in silence for a few minutes, and when they turned onto Seaside Lane, Meg said thoughtfully, "Odd, isn't it, how love can come in different ways? With you and Alix, the thunderbolt. With Dee and James, friendship blossoming into something richer."

Sam detected a faint wistfulness in her voice. The first sign of softening he'd seen in her. A chink in the armor? "How was it for you, Meg? For you and Andy's dad?"

She stumbled, but righted herself before he could reach out to help her. "Do you mind if we don't talk about that?"

The tenor of their conversation had changed, in the flash of a finger-snap. Any softening he'd seen in her—

if it really had been a softening—had hardened to ice, and the ice was in her tone, in the rigidity of her body.

"You're divorced," he said placatingly, "and you don't want to talk about him—that I can understand. What I don't understand is why you put that family portrait in Andy's room—and Andy obviously didn't understand it, either! What's going on, Meg?"

She marched determinedly forward like a soldier on parade. "Nothing's going—"

"I hate to see a kid so upset. Why would you hang his father's picture on his bedroom wall when you must have known that looking at his father would only hurt him? Hell, the guy walked out on him!"

They had reached the foot of the Carradines's driveway. She turned on him, her eyes sparking. "I said I don't want to discuss this with you! Will you please drop it?"

He raised his palms in surrender. "Consider it dropped."

Easy to say, he reflected somberly...but he knew he'd still think about the puzzle, try to figure it out. She couldn't stop him from doing that.

"Thank you! Now if you'll excuse me—" her tone was curt "—I have to go home and get my casseroles." She veered past him and started across the lawn.

He caught up with her. "I'll help."

"That's not necessary."

He ignored the rebuff and thought he heard a frustrated sigh which he decided, also, to ignore.

He glanced around the carport as they walked through it. A couple of bikes lay against the wall—one had a flat tire. That would be Meg's. He also noticed, among odds and ends on a wooden shelf, a repair kit. "I've never seen a car here," he murmured. "You and Dee don't drive?"

"We shared an old Volvo...but when it gave up the

ghost a month ago we didn't replace it. James plans on buying Dee a car when they get back from their honeymoon, and I can do without one. I either bike or walk now—used to do that most of the time anyway, even when we had the Volvo.''

She opened the screen door and as he followed her inside, he saw that Andy was in the kitchen.

He was cooking frozen pizzas in the toaster oven and on the table was a carton of orange juice and a tall glass.

"Hi, Mom—" He broke off when he saw his mother wasn't alone.

Sam ran an appraising gaze over the boy. He hadn't had much of a chance to do so that morning; Meg had wanted to talk to Andy alone and had sent him packing. He could see now that though the boy did have Meg's chiseled features, they were more strongly molded. His skin was tanned to a deep brown, making his eyes bluer than ever. His eyebrows were black, and his longish hair, wet from a shower or a swim, shone like polished jet. He had a scar on his brow, about an inch long, that disappeared into his hairline.

As he ripped up the pizza packet and stuffed it into the garbage under the sink, Sam's gaze was drawn to his hands. Lean capable-looking hands—very like his own; long-fingered with square nails, bluntly trimmed—

"We've come to pick up some casseroles for Elsa."

Meg's voice interrupted his scrutiny and when he glanced at her, he thought she looked flustered. Why? Was she remembering that Andy had caught them in a compromising position yesterday? What other reason could there be?

"Andy," she went on, "this is Mr. Grainger."

Features taut, Andy came forward and stuck out his right hand. "Hi."

So, Sam mused, the boy had manners…and didn't let his hostility override them. "Hi, Andy."

The boy had a firm grip but prolonged the handshake not a nanosecond longer than necessary.

Meg transferred the casseroles from fridge to table. "Aren't you coming to Elsa's for supper?" she asked Andy.

Sam's curiosity was further piqued when he noticed that her cheeks had become flushed, and her gaze seemed panicky as it darted from Andy to him and back again to Andy—like a mother bird hovering over her young in the nest, sensing danger. What was she looking for? What was she seeing?

What the devil was she afraid of?

The toaster oven pinged and Andy took out his pizzas. "Brad's coming over, we're going Rollerblading."

He sensed that with her son's announcement, some of her tension oozed away. Perhaps she hadn't wanted Andy to come to Elsa's. Was she afraid he might provoke another scene?

"Be home by ten-thirty," she said.

"Sure."

Sam took charge of a couple of the casserole dishes, Meg lifted the other two, and Andy moved to the door and held it open.

"Thanks," they both said.

"You're welcome."

Meg was silent on the way over to the Carradines's.

"Andy's a nice kid," Sam remarked as they approached the back door. "You must be proud of him."

"Yes, I'm *very* proud of him."

"What I'd give to have a son like that." He hadn't meant to say the words aloud, they'd just spilled out.

To his bewilderment, she tensed up again. And when she spoke, her tone had a grating edge. "We all have choices to make."

"Choices?"

"You said, the night of the barbecue, that you and

Alix had got caught up in the rat race. I interpreted that to mean you'd put the pursuit of the almighty dollar ahead of the pursuit of having children.'' She lifted her shoulders in a scornful fashion that implied *You can't have it both ways!* "As I said, we all make choices.''

He wanted to tell her, angrily, that the choice to remain childless had not been his, but had been made for him, with neither his knowledge nor consent, by his wife.

But he kept quiet.

It was none of her business.

But what she'd said had irritated him. It irritated him that she had judged him without knowing all the facts.

Yet why should it bother him that she thought badly of him on this particular issue? Heck, she thought badly of him on every issue that came up! He'd never met anyone with such volatile moods, such a hair-trigger temper—at least, as far as he was concerned.

He should have been pleased, then, that she made a point of staying out of his way both during and after the rehearsal dinner...

So why was it that he couldn't keep his eyes off her over the meal? Why was it that afterward, when they'd all adjourned to the sitting room for coffee, he was constantly aware of her—aware of her subtle peachy perfume when she glided past his chair, aware of her sweet smile as she passed cream and sugar to the minister, aware of the beguiling curve of her breasts as, finally seated on a low ottoman, she reached up to accept a mug of coffee from Dee?

It mystified him, just as *she* mystified him.

And as he listened with half an ear to the conversation humming around him, he found his gaze drawn, over and over again, to the slender figure in yellow, sitting straight-backed on the vinyl ottoman. With her hands curved around her floral china mug, her eyes alert and her smile at the ready, she looked as if she was enjoying herself thoroughly.

Only when her glance chanced to fall on him did he see a shadow darken her expression.

And when it did, it darkened something inside him, too.

And he hadn't the first clue as to why that should be.

"More coffee, Meg?"

"No, thanks, Elsa." Meg rose off the ottoman and, giving the older woman a hug, whispered, "It's been a lovely evening but if you don't mind, I'm going to slip away now."

"Sam's slipped away, too. Off to bed, I guess. The sea air makes everybody sleepy when they first come here."

Yes, Meg had noticed Sam leaving about ten minutes ago. She'd been glad. Relieved. She'd sensed him watching her all evening, and every time she'd looked at him, his eyes had been fixed on her gravely, prob-ingly...and apprehension had gripped her as she won-dered what he was thinking.

Was he thinking about...his hands?

And their similarity to...Andy's hands?

She had never noticed Sam's hands in the past; had never realized they were so like his son's. But *he* had noticed. She had seen him staring at Andy's hands when Andy was ripping up the pizza packet. Her heart had almost stopped—

"Have a good sleep," Elsa said. "Tomorrow's the big day—and it's going to be a day to remember!"

A day to remember.

The words roiled around in Meg's head as she closed Elsa's back door behind her. It would indeed be a day to remember—especially if Sam Grainger confronted her with suspicions about Andy's paternity. She exhaled a shuddering sigh as she walked through the gateway, a sigh that was cut off abruptly when she noticed the carport light was on. She saw the flicker of moving shadows. Her pulse stuttered.

"Andy?" she called out nervously as she turned the corner.

"No," came a deep sexy voice, "it's me."

Meg stopped in the entryway, and stared disbelievingly. Sam Grainger was crouched down on his haunches, a grimy smudge on one cheek, and she could see he had just completed the final stage of repairing her flat tire.

"There." His knees cracked as he stood, and he said with a grin, "Lord, hear that? I'm getting old, Beanpole."

In the white halogen light, she saw that a swath of his black hair had fallen forward; she watched, her breath caught, as he swept it back with one beautiful long-fingered hand. His grin tugged at her heart, startling her with a sudden yearning so achingly intense she felt weak.

Ever since Sam Grainger had come back into her life, she'd been dizzied by confusion—confusion caused by her conflicting feelings for him. Now, like a mist blown away by a cleansing gale, that confusion scattered and left her with a truth that shook her to her foundation.

She was in love with this man. Deeply, crazily, and terminally in love with him.

"I can see I've rendered you speechless!" Chuckling, he walked past her. "And that in itself is a small miracle. Good night, Meg. See you tomorrow in church!"

CHAPTER SIX

"WHAT a perfect day for a wedding!" Dee's eyes shone as she descended the stairs in her Victorian-style ivory lace gown. "I thought, when I woke up at seven and saw that rain—"

"Mmm, me, too." Following her sister downstairs, Meg hitched up the long straight skirt of her midnight-blue silk dress. "But now it's *gloriously* sunny!"

"You look terrific!" Dee called to Andy, who was preening at the hall mirror, proud as a peacock in his very first suit.

He turned and looked up at them. "Wow, Aunt Dee, *you* look like the cover of one of your *Bride* magazines! And you're not half bad, too, Mom." Andy grinned, and Meg almost closed her eyes as the smile slammed into her. Sam's smile.

Sam. Her stomach twisted into a knot even as her heart leaped. How was she going to get through today without giving away her secret? She'd seen women in love—women like Dee; she knew how they glowed. Did she glow, too? She prayed that if she did and anyone noticed, they would put it down to her happiness for her sister on this special day.

The front doorbell rang. Through the glass side panels, she saw Mark, who was going to give Dee away. As Andy opened the door, she saw Miranda Page, too, the professional photographer Dee had hired to take the wedding pictures.

She also caught a glimpse of the black Infiniti backing into the street. Sam had been out earlier that morning—she'd seen him leave in the direction of town as the florist's van arrived—but later, from her bedroom window, she'd seen him in the drive, washing the vehicle vigorously. Now he was off to church with the groom.

Dee led the small group out to her flower garden, where she wanted some informal pictures taken.

"Groom's gone," Miranda announced. "No chance he'll see you before the wedding, Dee!"

When she was finally satisfied with the photographs she'd snapped, Miranda left for the church in her Sprint, taking Andy with her. And right after that, two cars pulled up at the curb, a shiny black taxi to take Meg to the church, and a silver limo for Dee and Mark.

As Dee made one last quick trip up to the bathroom, Mark said to Meg, "Honey, I guess you've heard that I've sold the inn—just signed the deal this morning."

"No, I hadn't heard. Oh, Mark, I'm so pleased for you!" Meg gave him a hug. "That's wonderful." She managed to keep her feelings of anxiety from her voice, not wanting to spoil Mark's obvious happiness.

"Aye, Deborah and I are delighted. And you needn't worry about losing your promotion. I plan on talking to the new owner about that today, and I foresee no problems." His expression was puzzled. "I'm just surprised, Marguerite, that he hasn't told you the news himself! But I guess he's been real busy today, with all his duties."

"Nobody's told me anything! And how can you be so sure I'll keep my job, far less the promotion you promised me?"

"Because the man's a friend of yours. Heck, he told me you and Dee kindly put him up for a couple of nights, when Elsa didn't have his room ready."

No, she wasn't hearing correctly. Either that, or Mark was mistaken. Must be. Or else she had walked into the middle of a nightmare.

"Not...S...Sam Grainger?"

"That's the one!"

Disbelief blasted through Meg. Sam Grainger had bought the inn? No, it was impossible! Unthinkable. Untenable!

The man was a lawyer. He lived in Portland. He *worked* in Portland! He—

"Sorry to keep you waiting!" Long skirt hauled up so she didn't trip on the hem, Dee descended the stairs. "Off you go, Meg." She lifted her bouquet from the hall table. "Mark and I will give you a few minutes, then we'll follow."

"Right, Dee." Meg's smile belied her inner turmoil. "See you at the church!"

The smile wilted as she walked dazedly out to the taxi. Sam Grainger was the new owner of the Seashore Inn. Desperately she tried to come to grips with the news.

She'd counted on his leaving town tomorrow. She'd expected he'd then be out of her life again, forever this time, without having discovered the truth about Andy.

She slumped back in her seat as the taxi driver swept the vehicle from the curb. If Sam Grainger settled here in Seashore, she'd be seeing him almost every day. The only alternative was to give up her job and move somewhere else. But that was not an option. In the first place, with the job market the way it was, chances were she'd never get a position that paid as much as she'd make at the inn. In the second place, she'd be crazy to move Andy from Seashore just as he was ready to move into high school with the friends he'd grown up with. It would be a recipe for trouble.

No, she was stuck where she was.

She'd been afraid, last night, that Sam had suspected he might be Andy's father. That fear had been put to rest by his teasing attitude in the carport. But he was an observant man; how long would it be before he did latch onto the truth?

As for his wife—even if Alix Grainger didn't like small towns, if her husband made Seashore his home surely she'd come here to be with him between assignments.

She was a very smart woman. Would *she* spot the resemblances between her husband and Andy?

Meg felt as if the world was closing in on her. But what could she do about it?

Even as she asked herself the question, the taxi drew to a halt in front of the church, where a small crowd had gathered to await the arrival of the bride. With a huge effort, she shoved her anxieties to the back of her mind. This was Dee's wedding day. She had to concentrate on that.

She would worry about Sam Grainger later.

Easier said than done.

The wedding went off beautifully, but for Meg the whole ceremony seemed oddly removed. Oh, she saw Dee, James, and the minister; and she heard what they said; and she was cognizant of the fact that the church was packed, tastefully decorated, and smelled faintly of roses. But that all seemed distant. What did *not* seem distant, but immediate, was the best man...and of him she was *vibrantly* aware.

Like James, Sam Grainger was wearing a black tux. Unlike James, who looked endearingly sweet and humble and earnest, Sam looked incredibly elegant and dynamic and sexy. She *tried* to avoid glancing at him but on the two occasions when she surrendered to her debilitating need to feast her eyes on him, she found his gaze was already fixed on her.

The first time, he lowered one eyelid in a seductive half wink. She bit her lip and looked quickly away.

The next time she snuck a glance, his intense green eyes had a wicked twinkle as if he knew, absolutely knew, she hadn't been able to help herself. She felt a blush creep into her cheeks, and from then on, she focused her gaze, with a sense of quiet desperation, on the minister.

Walking down the aisle with him after the ceremony was sheer torture. As he'd done at the rehearsal, he tucked her arm firmly through his, and every step they took together sent a wave of shimmering heat through her.

Over the scent of roses, she smelled his spicy aftershave, male, musky…erotic. It sang to every carnal cell in her body, and by the time the wedding party emerged into the sunshine, her legs felt as dependable as a set of rubber stilts. She was thankful to escape from him as Miranda arranged everyone on the steps for photographs.

Afterward, it was time to leave for the reception, which was to be held at the Seashore Golf and Country Club, a few miles inland. Since it was Sam's duty to drive her there, she found herself at his mercy again.

As he settled her into the Infiniti's passenger seat, he said cheerily, "The wedding went well, didn't it!"

"Yes, very well."

"The bride was beautiful, but you looked positively ravishing."

Ravishing? Oh, yes…ravishing had *certainly* been on her mind. And still was! "I am not—" she clutched her hands together to keep herself from reaching up and clutching *him* "—into flirting with married men."

He slammed the door and rounded the car.

As he pulled away, he said, "I wasn't *flirting*. I was merely paying you a compliment."

"You can keep that kind of compliment," she said with a glance that would have cut steel, "for your wife."

She'd annoyed him. She could see it in his quick frown. Well, good. If a reminder that he was married would make him watch his mouth, then she would bear that in mind.

But...she did need to talk to him. She had to find out what he intended to do with the inn. And it was imperative that she ask him before they reached the clubhouse and got swallowed up in the crowd at the reception.

She waited till they were almost there, before turning in her seat and saying abruptly, "Mark tells me you've bought the inn."

"He told you?" He kept his eyes the road. "Well, I guess it had to come out sooner or later..."

"*Why?*"

"You can't keep something like that a secret for long. At least not in a small town like—"

"I meant, why did you buy it!"

"Because the time was right."

"Did you buy it as an investment?"

"Well, sure...it's an investment..."

She felt as if an overwhelming weight had been lifted from her shoulders. And she couldn't keep the relief from her voice as she said, "Of course. So you'll remain in Portland and hire someone to run the inn."

"Heck, no! I'm going to sell my shares in the firm, cut myself off from it completely. I plan on moving here, making Seashore my home."

Shock rippled through her. And when he glanced at her, he could obviously read it in her face.

He quirked an eyebrow. "You have a problem with that?"

Oh, yes, she had a problem with that—a *huge* problem. But he must never know. She scrambled in her mind for an explanation that would explain away her dismay. And she grasped at one that had some truth in it. "It's...just that...well, you know I work there. At the inn. The present assistant manager—Mark's fiancée—is retiring next month. Mark had promised me the job after she leaves.''

They were approaching the turnoff for the country club. Sam slowed, and wheeled the car onto the private road. ''And you're concerned,'' he said slowly, ''that I may not honor that agreement.''

''You...you're not bound to.'' She smoothed a nervous hand over her midnight-blue dress, ironing it over her knees. ''Mark said he'd talk to you about it. But...I'm not asking for any favors. After the way I've been behaving,'' she added in a low voice, ''I'll quite understand if you don't want to keep me on.''

''I'll talk with Mark. If he thinks you can handle the job, that'll be good enough for me.'' They'd reached the parking lot, and drawing in to a vacant spot near the building's entrance, he switched off the ignition.

''Meg.'' He turned toward her. ''About what happened earlier...the flirting, as you called it...you were—''

Someone rapped on her window, and when she looked round she saw Andy. She thanked heaven for the interruption; the last thing she wanted was to get into a discussion with Sam Grainger that might lead to her giving away her feelings for him.

''I'd better go,'' she said in a rush. ''Thanks for the drive.'' Over a sudden lump in her throat, she added, ''And congratulations. The inn's a grand old place as well as a good going concern. I'm sure you and Alix will be very happy there, when she comes home between assignments.''

She made to open the door.

''Meg...''

She paused, her hand on the door handle. Sam's face was set in serious lines. His eyes were very thoughtful, as if he had just come to a decision. He leaned toward her a little, and when he spoke again, she found her gaze drawn, hypnotically, inexorably, helplessly, to his lips.

"Keep this to yourself," he murmured. "I don't want it to get out before James and Dee have left. Alix won't be coming to the inn. We've split up, Meg. Permanently. Our divorce became final earlier this week."

The bride's bouquet was a charming arrangement of cream roses, pink freesia, and baby's breath.

Dee laughed as she tossed it toward the wedding guests who had clustered outside the country club, in the gathering dark, to wish the married couple bon voyage.

Meg had already said her goodbyes to Dee and James; now she stood at the back of the crowd, still trying to cope with the anguish and indecision that had been tearing her heart for the past several hours.

Sam Grainger is free.

Mercilessly the words pounded her brain...and with the words came the hammering command of her conscience, You *must* tell him now about his son. His marriage is over. That obstacle to the truth no longer exists—

Meg ducked and put up a hand to protect herself as something came flying toward her from above.

And only when she found she was holding Dee's bouquet, and at the same time heard the cheers and shouts from the crowd, did she realize what she'd done.

Gathering herself together with an effort, she faked a bright smile...and saw that her sister looked jubilant.

Then Dee and James were in James's car and the car was gliding away down the drive.

Meg wondered if she'd ever felt more desolate.

"So...your turn next!"

She didn't glance round as Sam's amused voice came to her from behind her left shoulder.

"Definitely not," she said. "Once was enough."

She watched the car's rear lights disappear into the night, watched the guests return in gaily chatting groups. From inside came the head-pounding beat of music as the band struck up again, with "'Rock Around the Clock.'" She sensed that Sam had stayed put, that he was waiting for her. The other guests made their way inside, some of them stopping to say a word or two to her as they passed.

When they'd all gone, she finally turned to him.

"Look," she said, "your duties are over. You don't have to hang around with me. Go back in, enjoy the dance."

"How about you?"

"I'm going to stay out here for a bit."

"Are you feeling OK?"

"I need to get away from the music for a while. I'm going to take a walk. You could do me a favor, though."

"Sure."

She held out Dee's bouquet. "Would you take this inside? I'll pick it up later, when I'm ready to go home."

He took the bouquet, but instead of taking off up the steps into the clubhouse, he strode over to his car, which was parked nearby. Opening the trunk, he deposited it inside before slamming the lid down again.

"Since I'm driving you home—" he strolled back to her "—it'll be handier to leave the flowers in my car."

"You don't have to drive me home."

"I want to."

She sketched a defeated gesture. But before she could drop her hand, he'd caught it in one of his.

"Right," he said. "Let's walk."

She resisted, but only for a second. She didn't have the energy to struggle against him...and besides, she really did need to get away from the ear-splitting music. Her head had started to pound painfully in time to the beat.

She allowed him to lead her across the paved fore-court and around the side of the building. They walked past the pro shop, then across a wooden pathway rutted by golf spikes, and finally onto the manicured grass of the course.

Keeping off the eighteenth green, they rounded it to the top of the fairway, which was illuminated by the halogen lights directed over the nearby practice putting green.

"It's been a tough day for you, hasn't it?" Sam gave her hand a gentle squeeze. "You're going to miss Dee."

"Yes, I'll miss her." Missed her already, actually. She and Dee had talked while Dee was changing into her going-away outfit, but because Sam had specifically requested that she not tell Dee or James about his di-vorce, she'd been unable to pour out her anxieties, un-able to ask her sister for advice. Her voice caught as she went on, "But I know she and James are going to be happy."

"Yeah." He squeezed her hand again, comfort-ingly...and she had to fight a smarting of tears. This compassionate side of him...she found it hard to deal with. Or maybe it was just that she was especially vul-nerable today, what with everything that had been going on.

They walked on in silence, and the farther they walked from the clubhouse, the more shadowy their sur-roundings became. Ahead was a pond, its black surface glittering in the starlight.

Meg winced as the pain in her head became vicious.

"What's up?" Sam asked, halting.

She grimaced. "Just a headache."

"Tension headache." He released her hand and moved behind her. "Stand still." Before she could guess what he intended, he'd started massaging the muscles just above her shoulder blades.

After a moment's automatic resistance, Meg gave in. How could she not? What should she say, Don't touch me because I'm putty in your hands? Hardly.

So she tried to relax, and let him get at it. And after a minute or so, she heard herself give a long sigh. It felt so good. He knew just where to knead, knew just where the muscles were knotted.

She closed her eyes as his hands moved to her neck. He slid his long fingers under the string of pearls that had been the bride's present and proceeded to massage her in an impersonal way that seemed entirely unthreatening, and at last she felt her tension start to ease.

"Do you mind," he asked in a while, "if I take these flowers from your hair?"

"Uh-uh…"

He plucked off the circlet of miniature roses. She heard a rustle and imagined him tucking the headpiece into his jacket pocket. Then his fingers were in her hair, sifting through it like silk as he massaged her skull.

Bliss. Sheer bliss.

"That feels wonderful," she murmured. Whatever he was doing to her, it was working. And as her headache gradually dissipated, she became physically aware, in a different way, of the man standing so close to her, his fingers working their tender magic now on her temples…

Stroking, caressing, soothing.

She sighed again, and gave herself totally up to his skillful ministrations, no longer concentrating on the healing aspect of his touch, but on the excitingly sensual aspect. Her whole body was melting, like honey in the sun. She wanted to lean back against him, wanted him to put his arms around her, hold her close. She closed her eyes, let her imagination run away with her. Dreaming. Wishing…

And after what seemed like a heavenly eternity, when he slid his hands to her shoulders and turned her around, she opened her eyes, startled as if suddenly coming awake—and almost moaned aloud in protest.

"There." He looked down at her. "Better?"

She felt breathless, stunned by his hard male beauty. In the starlight, his face was alabaster angles and ebony shadows; his eyes narrowed slits, his mouth a temptation. In the night air, his pheromones were musk and spice and much more than nice...

Male scents, that drew her and beguiled her and threatened to overcome her, as they had done, so easily, that long-ago night.

She shivered, and the ripple ran from the tip of her head to the tips of her toes. That long-ago night had been a mistake. A mistake she must never make again.

"Hey, you're cold." He swung off his jacket and draped it over her shoulders. "Let's get back."

He clasped her wrist, and guided her back up the fairway, their footsteps rustling on the short dry grass. His attitude was friendly, nothing more. It seemed that though his caresses had left her weak and shaken, touching her had not had the same effect on him.

And thank heaven for that. If he'd wanted her as much as she wanted him, right now they'd be lying on the grass, kissing as if there was no tomorrow.

She inhaled a deep breath, banished the dangerous image, and looked up at him. "I was distressed," she said, "to hear you and your wife had broken up."

"Water under the bridge. And to echo what you said earlier, 'Once was enough.'"

"So you won't get married again?" Why did she bother to ask the question? He had already given her the answer.

"No way! Whoever said love was blind didn't know the half of it. But I've got the blinkers off now and I'll run like hell from any woman who wants an emotional commitment."

Meg wished she wasn't so conscious of his fingers on her wrist, or the warm spicy scent of him from his jacket...

Wished she hadn't fallen in love with this man, who was so vehemently opposed to emotional commitment.

When they reached the eighteenth green, they once again rounded it. As they walked across the path, Sam said, "You must be tired. D'you want to call it a day?"

"Yes. If you don't mind?"

"I've just got a couple of things to do inside first, pay the band and so on. When will you be ready to leave?"

"Soon as I collect Dee's wedding dress."

"What about Andy?" He slipped his jacket from her shoulders and put it on.

"He and Mike left earlier. Miranda drove them home."

As they walked into the foyer, Meg noticed the band was playing "The Tennessee Waltz." Dreamy. Nostalgic.

Heartbreaking.

Sam took her headpiece from his pocket and with a concentrated frown, he carefully arranged it on her hair again. His fingers lingered on her shoulders and his dark green eyes linked with hers.

"Fancy a dance?" he asked.

A tremor ran through her. To be in his arms? To dance to that song? She couldn't think of anything she'd like more. "No, thanks—but stay if you want, I can get a cab."

"I'm ready to leave." He dropped his hands and gave her an easy smile. "See you back here in ten minutes."

As they left the country club, Meg sat stiffly in the car, excruciatingly aware of Sam's closeness. They weren't touching, but even so her skin prickled and before long she felt beads of perspiration trickling down between her breasts. Breasts that felt swollen and tender...

He started humming. "The Tennessee Waltz." Achingly, she stared at the road ahead, watched hedges and trees flash by, briefly illuminated by the headlights, and tried not to listen to him, not to think about him.

Impossible.

On the outskirts of Seashore, she saw a rabbit freeze on the graveled shoulder, eyes shining like laser-bright buttons. Hypnotized. Her mouth twisted self-derisively. She could relate to that feeling...

When Sam parked the car in her drive, she got out before he had time to reach over and open her door. She hurried round to the trunk and when he opened it, she lifted out Dee's bouquet. He hauled out the bulky box containing Dee's dress, and another large one with her accoutrements.

Meg could see it would be impossible for her to carry everything in by herself, so she had no option but to take the lead and precede him along the path to the back door.

In the kitchen she found a note on the table. *Sleeping over at Mike's, see you tomorrow. Luv A.*

"Problem?" Sam asked as he dumped his boxes on a chair.

"It's from Andy. He's sleeping over at a friend's."

"So you'll be alone here tonight."

Meg gave a light laugh. "The first time in memory! So...can I offer you a nightcap?" She hoped he'd say no; she hoped he'd say yes. Her head swirled as it tried unsuccessfully to make sense of *what* she wanted!

"Sure. Thanks."

Now she wished he'd said "No"! "Hot chocolate?"

"That'd be great."

He loosened his black bow tie, undid the top buttons

of his ruffled shirt. Sitting down at the table, he stretched out his long legs. He looked as relaxed as she felt tense.

"So," he said idly, "did Dee tell you where they were going on their honeymoon?"

"No. Did James tell you?"

"Nope."

As they sipped their drinks, the small talk lapsed. She slipped off her sandals, flexed her toes. After a while, he said, "Mark and I had a chat. You don't have to worry about your job, Meg. He has absolute faith in your abilities to take over the assistant manager's post."

"That's wonderful news." She hesitated and then said, "I promise you'll find me easy to work with."

"I'm looking forward to it."

"When are you taking over?"

"First of October." He finished his cocoa, and getting up, slotted his mug in the dishwasher.

He peered out the window into the darkness. "Nobody home yet, next door. I guess Elsa's still whooping it up."

"Yes," Meg said, "she does love to dance!" Rising, she padded in her stockinged feet to look out the window.

Sam turned, but obviously hadn't heard her cross to stand at his shoulder, and he bumped into her, almost knocking her over. He grabbed her, swung her upright again.

And didn't release her.

"We really have to stop bumping like this!" he said, his eyes twinkling. Then his gaze dropped to her parted lips and his eyes no longer twinkled.

He took in a deep breath. He wanted to kiss her. She looked so sweet...so enticingly sweet. Her lips were dewy, pink, full...and inviting.

He tightened his grip on her arms.

She wasn't struggling.

He pulled her closer. Her breasts tipped against his chest, her pelvis brushed his thighs.

When he'd worked on her headache earlier, he'd become aroused. Fully aroused. But he'd restrained himself because he'd known how vulnerable she was at that point. And she was *still* vulnerable. It had been an exhausting day for her, and he wasn't about to take advantage of that fact.

But one quick kiss…what was the harm?

Sliding his hands up into her hair, he tilted her head to get better access to her mouth.

He'd meant the kiss to be light—a casual good-night kiss. And it might have ended up that way if he hadn't heard her throaty whimper as he brushed his lips against hers. It caught him off balance, but before he could draw away, she'd twined her arms around his neck and was kissing him back with a fervent passion that set his blood sizzling.

He was no slouch when it came to returning kiss for kiss, and by the time they came up for air, his heart was hammering and his senses were aflame.

Suppressing a groan, he drew back and looked down into her uptilted face. Her eyes were closed, her skin flushed, her lips swollen and parted…

He stared. Mesmerized. She looked so young, he thought wonderingly. So…innocent.

Deep deep inside him, a memory stirred. He frowned. The oddest feeling swept over him. A feeling of déjà vu.

He'd looked at her like this before, he'd kissed her like this before…sometime in the past.

No, that was *ridiculous*! He'd never held her like this before—he'd never kissed her before. For Pete's sake, the last time he'd seen her, she'd been only thirteen or fourteen. Just a kid. He'd barely known she existed in those days. Beanpole. The lanky kid who lived next door to James, the one with her shoulders slouched and her face always half hidden by a sweep of untidy long hair.

He shook his head. Tried to shake off the feeling of familiarity, but still it persisted—

And oddly, inexplicably, it *chilled* him.

Meg's eyes were open. Wide. They locked with his. She stiffened. And then he felt her flinch from him.

What the *hell* had she seen in his expression?

Before he could begin to guess, she had slipped free.

She walked—unsteadily—to the outside door and opened it. "It's late." Her face was suffused with color. "Thanks for...being my escort, and for taking me home."

He raked a hand through his hair. Did he look as stunned and shocked as he felt? He hoped not. But the chilled sensation persisted; it seemed to reach right into him—into his very soul, encasing it in ice. He rubbed a hand against his chest, but the feeling remained.

He cleared his throat, but when he spoke, his voice still came out huskily. "No problem. Will I see you tomorrow? At Elsa's out-of-towners brunch?"

"Yes," she said. "I'll be there."

"I'll be leaving right after." He crossed to stand in the doorway, beside her. Her scent came to him, but his desire to make love to her had gone, killed by the coldness inside him. "Good night then. You'll be OK on your own?"

She nodded. "I'll be fine."

He walked past her, into the night. And as he went, he said softly over his shoulder, "Sweet dreams."

CHAPTER SEVEN

SWEET dreams indeed!

Meg smiled bleakly as she walked over to Elsa's next morning; after Sam's chilling rejection of her, how could he have expected she'd even *sleep*. She flushed with shame at memory of his shocked expression. He'd obviously intended his kiss to be only a casual good-night one but instead of responding in kind, she'd whimpered pathetically and flung herself at him with all the finesse of a rutting goat!

She blew out a despairing sigh. After tossing and turning for half the night, she'd spent the other half curled up on her window seat, staring wretchedly over the starlit sea and agonizing over her conflicting feelings.

Bad enough that she was in love with a man who didn't want to get emotionally involved, but how could she be in love with a man who had treated her so badly in the past—a man, for Pete's sake, with no *conscience*.

That character flaw stained him so deeply in her eyes that she was at a complete loss to understand herself— to understand how she could be so besotted with him. So hopelessly infatuated.

So...lovesick.

She paused in the gateway and set a hand on the fence post. Yes, she thought, with dawning understanding, that was it: she was love*sick*. She'd never realized the expression could be taken literally, but in her case it was apt. She felt faint and dizzy and off-kilter—and strangely detached...as if she was no longer part of the real world.

But she *was* part of that world...and so was Sam. And

today, before he left, no matter what, she had to tell him about Andy.

It would have been difficult enough before, she reflected as she moved on into Elsa's yard, but after what had happened last night, the task ahead seemed overwhelming. Would she be able to hide her love for Sam as she told him he was the father of her child?

She prayed she would. How unbearably humiliating it would be to reveal the secrets of her heart to this man who had sworn never again to give his to any woman—

"Good morning!" Elsa called from the back door. "You're the first to arrive. Just what I need, an extra pair of hands! Everybody's deserted me!"

Meg followed Elsa inside. "I'd love to help. But...where's Sam?" He *had* to be here—she'd screwed up her courage to talk to him; if he'd already left, her courage would leave, too, and she doubted she'd ever find it again.

Elsa drew a tray of sizzling mini quiches from the oven. "Would you carry those punch glasses through to the dining room, dear?" She set the tray on a trivet on the table. "Sam drove down to the corner store to get me a tub of ice cream—oh, there's the front doorbell!" Elsa scurried out of the kitchen to welcome the new arrivals.

Meg was just about to lift the tray of punch glasses when the back door opened and Sam ambled in. Like her, he was dressed in a casual shirt and shorts. Unlike her, he looked as if he'd slept the night through. His eyes were bright as washed emeralds—and she felt a wave of relief when she saw nothing in them to make her think he was remembering the night before.

"Hi!" he said cheerfully. "I was looking for you on the beach this morning. What happened? You sleep in?"

He made for the fridge and crouched down to tuck the ice cream into the bottom drawer of the freezer section. Meg stared at him…and braced herself against his magnetism. This man wasn't into commitment. She had to keep reminding herself of that. He might have been shocked at her wanton response last night, but he was only human…and next time, instead of being taken by surprise, he might just accept what was offered. Did she really want a repeat of thirteen years ago, when she'd given herself to him only to have him cast her aside after like a used tissue?

He straightened, and automatically she stepped back, wrapping protective arms around herself.

He raised his eyebrows. ''Did you?''

''What?''

''Sleep in.''

''Oh…no, I didn't sleep too well, actually, and I couldn't seem to find enough energy to go jogging.'' Before her courage had time to fail, she went on in a rush, ''Sometime before you leave, I need to talk to you.''

''How about now? I'm all ears!''

Laughter wafted in from the corridor. Then Elsa's voice. ''Well we can't have punch without glasses! Meg was supposed to bring them through…but you just can't get good help nowadays!''

''Heck, I'd fire her!'' somebody called.

Hoots of laughter.

''Andy.'' Elsa's voice again. ''Would you run through to the kitchen and light a fire under your mom?''

Footsteps. Approaching.

Andy's familiar tread.

''Alone,'' Meg said quickly to Sam. ''What I have to say to you is private. We can…take a walk along the beach.''

He cocked an eyebrow. ''Intriguing!''

Andy burst in, but skidded to a halt when he saw Sam.

''Good morning,'' Sam said.

"Hi." Andy turned his attention to his mother. "Mom, you're supposed to bring through the glasses."

Meg lifted the tray, but nervousness had her hands shaking so badly the glasses tinkled against each other.

Sam relieved her of the tray. "I'll get this," he said. And as Andy watched with a scowl marring his brow, he murmured, "Later, then. Right after we've eaten?"

She nodded.

He took off.

Meg threw Andy a tight smile, and with a pair of tongs busied herself arranging the mini quiches on a warmed platter. "Did you enjoy the wedding?"

"Why's that jerk still hanging around you?"

"Mr. Grainger's not hanging around *me*. He was in the kitchen because Elsa sent him to the store for ice cream."

Belligerently, he said, "What's going on? Why does he want to see you later, after you've eaten?"

Meg stilled. "Andy," she said carefully, "he doesn't want to see me. It's the other way around. I...need to talk to him about something. Something...private—"

His face darkened further. "How come you're having secrets with him? You said you didn't even like him!"

"It's not a question of liking or not liking—"

Andy wheeled round and made for the door.

She caught him by the sleeve of his shirt and stopped him. "Honey," she said quietly, "don't get upset. After Mr. Grainger has left, I want to talk to you, too. I'll tell you all about it. I promise."

After the brunch, Meg couldn't have said if she'd eaten quiche or cardboard. Her mind had not been on her food.

Sam, however, had filled his plate and eaten with gusto. He'd looked as if didn't have a care in the world.

And now, as they left Elsa's for their previously arranged walk, she saw him inhale a deep breath of pleasure. The afternoon was warm, with a tangy breeze wafting in from the ocean—and she guessed he was thinking that a stroll by the water would set him up nicely for his long drive home.

Little did he know what lay just ahead of him.

"So...which way?" He cupped Meg's elbow firmly as they crossed the road and then brushed through the long salt grass. "To the inn or the marina?"

The beach, to the north, was busy with people. The southern stretch was comparatively quiet.

"Let's walk toward the inn."

When they reached the sand, Sam released her elbow, and as they fell into step together, Meg snuck him a sideways glance. His expression was thoughtful. Was he wondering what she wanted to talk to him about? Did he think it had something to do with her job? That she needed reassurance regarding her promotion? If only it were that simple...

Ahead of them, three teenagers were tossing a Frisbee around. As it landed in front of Sam, he whisked it up and tossed it back. Once they'd passed the trio, she said, "Are you in a hurry to leave? I know you have a long drive ahead—"

"I'm in no hurry."

"Then let's walk as far as the inn."

"Sure."

They hiked on, with little in the way of conversation, till they finally reached the tree where Meg had been sitting when she'd first spotted the For Sale sign.

Sam nodded toward the sign, with its new Sold sticker. "Mark didn't warn you, did he, that he was going to sell?"

"No, it all happened so quickly." She shook her head abstractedly. "But that's not what I want to talk about."

"No?" He planted his feet apart. "Then what?"

The breeze drifted a leaf down from the tree and she

felt it settle lightly on her head. She raised her hand to brush it away with her fingertips and her arm felt heavy as lead. Her cheeks felt as if the blood was draining from them; she wondered if they looked as ashen as they felt—

"Meg?" he prodded, his expression puzzled.

"This is going to be a shock to you." She swallowed convulsively. "I...this is so hard for me..."

He frowned. "Whatever it is, spit it out! Are you in some kind of trouble? Look, I'll do whatever I can to help you out. Do you need money? What the hell is it?"

She turned her back on him, and facing the tree trunk, began picking agitatedly at the bark.

He grasped her shoulders and turned her around.

She saw concern in his eyes and it brought a blur of tears to her own.

The concern darkened to apprehension. "What is it, Meg? For God's sake, tell me!"

Closing her eyes briefly, tightly, to squeeze the tears away, she made a huge effort to calm herself, and when she pulled back from him, he dropped his hands to his sides.

Somewhere in the distance a gull cried. And from the inn came a jarring echo of merry laughter.

Meg forced herself to meet his gaze. And keep it there. "You...have to understand...I couldn't tell you this before..." The words came out haltingly. "...I didn't want to do anything that might...wreck your marriage—"

"Meg, get to the point! What the *hell* could you possibly have said or done to wreck my marriage?"

This was it, then. The moment she'd been dreading for years, the moment that deep in her heart she'd known, had always known, was probably inevitable. He was waiting now, with his green eyes narrowed, wary.

She drew in a quivering breath and twisting her hands together, pressed them against her knotted stomach.

"I guess it's not every day," she whispered, "that a man finds out he's a father."

He stared at her blankly. Obviously not taking it in.

"Sam." Her voice trembled, and she heard the pleading in it as she went on to tell him the news that she knew would shake him to the very core. "Andy is your son."

Sam rocked back on his heels as if she'd slapped him.

But the shock and disbelief that had exploded through his mind gave way, swiftly, to white-hot anger; and the concern he'd been feeling for her gave way, too, just as swiftly, to an ice-cold wrath.

He rammed his fists against his hips and glared at her. "Just what scam are you trying to pull here, Meg?" His tone was harsh with fury. "What the *hell* are you up to?"

"It's no *scam.*" Tears glimmered in her eyes, glinted on her pale cheeks. "Andy. He's...yours." She made a beseeching gesture with her hands. *"Ours."*

"You're out of your mind. I don't know what your game is, but you're living in the past, Meggie mine!" His mouth curled with distaste. "Maybe a woman could have pulled this off fifteen, twenty years ago—but now with DNA your case would be laughed out of court."

"I don't need DNA." She'd gone from pleading to fury in two seconds flat. A feverish pink painted her chalky cheeks, a violent resentment flashed in her eyes. *"He looks more like you every day!"* The words tumbled out of her, condemnation accentuating every syllable. "You've noticed it yourself—even his hands, they're just like yours!"

"Oh, for God's sake!" He spun away from her and started striding back the way they'd come, his heavy steps making the ground reverberate. Without looking back, he shouted, "We both have dark hair and long fingers, but so have a few gazillion other guys on this planet!"

He heard her storming after him. He quickened his stride. When she caught up with him she snatched the back of his shirt, dug her heels in and put the brakes on him, though he pulled her into a skid as he tried to keep going.

He swung free of her, and whirled round. "You're sick, Meg. You'd better see a—"

"Don't run, damn you!" Meg glowered up at him. "You can't ignore me this time, Sam Grainger, the way you did after you used me and cast me aside thirteen years ago!"

He gawked at her. The woman was crazy. Cursing loudly and vehemently, he jammed his fists on his hips again.

"OK," he gritted out. "Lay it on me, the whole fabricated story."

"Fabricated story?" Her voice was high with disbelief. "Are you *still* going to pretend that night never happened?"

He rolled his eyes skyward, in a mute plea for guidance. Or deliverance. Or anything, as long as it got him out of this incredible, bizarre situation. "And what night might that be, Meg?"

"You know full well!"

He felt the last of his self-control begin to slip away. He hung on to it, but just barely. "Remind me," he said with soft menace.

She straightened her spine. "The night we had sex," she said. "You and I. On this very spot. Are you…going to deny it?"

"Deny it? How could I not deny it! It never happened. Except maybe in your adolescent fantasies!" Under-

standing suddenly dawned. ''Jeez, Elsa told me you had
a crush on me when you were fourteen but—''

''I was eighteen when it happened and you *know* it.
I'd just started working here at the inn that night—the
night you thought Alix had been killed abroad. I was
leaving for home after my shift and when I saw you
down by the water, in the moonlight, I went down there,
too, because I wanted to say hi. I had no idea what had
happened.'' He heard her voice catch. ''You were...
crying.''

He froze. What the...?

For a long, long moment he stared at her. He felt
shaken, off balance...as if the world, under his feet, had
just tilted. What was she *saying*? And what was he thinking! The...unthinkable.

He drew in a rasping breath. ''Go on,'' he said in a
gravelly voice he barely recognized as his own.

''You...know what happened.''

''Tell me.''

''We...you told me Alix was dead. I tried to comfort
you. We came up here.'' She stumbled. Her cheeks were
now red as fire. ''We...both thought Alix was—'' She
stopped and took in a ragged breath. ''But next morning,
you discovered the report had been mistaken, she wasn't
dead—though she was ill and in hospital, and you immediately took off for there.'' She turned away from
him, and stared out over the ocean. ''We'd had...sex.
Here...on the beach. But you never even called me—''
she tripped on the words ''—in case I might have gotten
pregnant.''

The waves smashed up the shore, frothing, and were
sucked back again by the tide. A gull shrieked by, its
call fierce and high. Sam wasn't sure just how long he
stood there, feeling numb and totally drained, before he
spoke. When he did, his voice was so low as to be almost
inaudible.

"Dear God." His words sounded like a desperate prayer. "Meggie...I didn't know."

He struggled to keep his mind from shattering as disconnected thoughts flew through it from all sides. He hung on to one: he had a son.

And as he clutched it, clutched it to his heart, he felt his heart stagger from the load...and from the almost overwhelming compassion he now felt for Meg, who had carried this burden without him, for...thirteen long years.

She was still staring out to sea. "You knew we'd had sex," she whispered. "Did it never occur to you that—"

"I have no memory of it, Meg—"

He heard a sharp in-hiss of breath. Then she whispered, at last, in a voice raw with pain, "Was I so forgettable, Sam?"

And he knew, then, just how very much he had hurt her.

"Oh, God, no, Meg, that's not what I mean." He ached to reach out to her, but first he had to explain. "You know I came here to convalesce—I was on powerful medication—and that night, when I heard Alix had been killed, I tried to drown my sorrows in vodka. I felt so damned helpless! There wasn't even a body—the report had announced there were no survivors, and with the explosion being over the Medi—" He winced as he recalled how he'd felt then. "At any rate, the mix of medication and alcohol did me in. I had a blackout. When I woke, the last thing I remembered of the previous evening was having room service send up a bottle of vodka. I switched on the TV first thing that morning to see what fresh news there might be of the explosion...and that's when I heard that Alix was alive—"

He halted as she turned. Slowly turned. Her eyes were glazed, her lips parted, her expression as groggy and incredulous as if he'd punched her.

"A...blackout? You had a...*blackout*?"

"Yeah." The word sighed out of him, and in that one word lay all his anguish, his regret, his remorse. "Yeah, Meggie. I remember nothing of our...time together."

She made a sound halfway between a hysterical laugh and a sob.

He still wanted to touch her, but was afraid to now. She seemed so fragile. So vulnerable. So wounded.

And he had no right to touch her.

Had never had any right...

"Why didn't you contact me?" he asked huskily. "When you discovered you were pregnant?"

She lifted her shoulders in an infinitely weary gesture. "How could I? You and Alix were happy. Such a thing—fathering an illegitimate child—could have ruined your marriage...

"I don't think that what we did was morally wrong," she went on, her tone strained as if she wanted to believe what she was saying but hadn't fully resolved the issue in her own mind. "We both believed Alix was dead, you were mourning your loss, I was trying to give you comfort...but if Alix had known of our encounter and especially since it had led to a child...it might have spoiled things between you. I decided not to take that risk."

Right now, Sam reflected, was not the time to wonder what would have happened between him and Alix if he'd known he had a son.

Andy.

An image of the boy rose vividly in his mind, and with it came a resurgence of the elation that had soared through him at the discovery he was a father. But mixed with his joy, and his worry about Meg, was deep concern for his son.

"Have you told Andy?" he asked. "About...this?"

"Nobody knows except Dee. I plan on telling Andy tonight."

"What then?"

"You'll be in Portland for the next month. When you come back, we can...talk again."

"I want to be part of my son's life." He saw her eyelids flicker. "If he wants that, too. I know he thinks I'm some kind of a jerk...but...maybe in time, I can win him over."

"We'll talk when you come back."

"Meg." He made to touch her arm but she pulled back. "I'm sorry. Sorry you had to—"

"It's history," she said. "But now that it's going to be out in the open, my first priority is Andy." She ran a shaky hand through her hair. "I just don't know how he's going to react to the news that you're his father."

If only Dee were here.

Meg looked up at the stars as she swayed back and forth on the swinging love seat in her backyard.

Had her sister been here, at least Andy would have had someone to turn to when he'd so violently rejected her after she'd told him Sam Grainger was his father.

She sighed. She'd tried to break the news gently, but it had all gone awry.

She'd taken Andy out for dinner to his favorite pizza place; then they'd gone to the skateboard bowl and she'd watched him swoop and gyrate and leap, giving him the thumbs-up every time he eagerly looked her way for approval.

They'd walked home together, in the gathering dusk, and as they walked, she'd told him. Omitting nothing. She'd highlighted Sam's blackout, and her own remorse for having misjudged him so sorely. Her tears had almost choked her as she spoke of how badly she'd treated Sam since his return to Seashore, when he'd done absolutely nothing to deserve the contempt she'd heaped on him.

Andy had spoken not one word while she filled him in. They were approaching the foot of their drive just as she came to the end of her story, and she finished by telling him that Sam had bought the inn and would be coming back to Seashore, for good, in one month's time.

She halted at the end of the drive.

"Andy, I know this has all been a terrible shock to you. You've always wanted to know who your father was—and now you can understand why it had to be such a secret. When I found out about Sam and Alix's divorce, found out your father was free, that set *me* free to tell you everything."

He wouldn't look at her.

"Andy—" She reached out to him but he lunged away from her, taking off across the road and onto the now-darkening beach. "Andy!" she called after him, and took a few steps across the road before halting.

He needed time alone. Time to think. And she had to give him that.

But now—Meg brushed up the sleeve of her shirt and glanced at her watch—it was past midnight and he still hadn't come home.

Where was he?

Her stomach had been twisted in a gnarled knot ever since he'd taken off. Now it twisted further. Oh, God, she hoped he wouldn't do something stupid. She hoped—

Her heart lurched as she heard the crunch of steps on the graveled drive.

Sliding off the swing, she stood there, her heart in her mouth.

Seconds later, she saw a shadowy figure come around the corner. A familiar figure, carrying a skateboard.

Relief almost swamped her.

"Oh, Andy." Her throat felt tight. "Where have you been? I was so worried—"

"Sorry." He kept walking, past her, toward the back door. He didn't let his eyes alight on her. "You don't have to worry about me. I'm OK. Hey, it's really cool that Sam Grainger's my dad. He's got pots of money. We'll be on easy street from now on in!"

His flippant tone, the rigidity of his figure, the averting of his eyes—all spelled out his distress...and his continued rejection of her.

Meg slumped down again onto the swing set, pain, anxiety, and compassion vying for upper place inside her.

Oh, Dee, she whispered, I so badly need someone to talk to. I so badly need advice on how to handle this.

But it might be weeks before she'd see her sister again. James and his bride were not returning to Seashore after their honeymoon, they were going straight to Seattle to settle in their new home.

Angrily Meg swiped away a threatening tear. Tears were going to solve nothing. She had to be *strong*, and she had to be *wise*.

She who had never considered herself to be either!

"It's all finally settled," Sam said to James. "I've sold my interest in the firm."

James looked shrewdly across his dining table at Sam. "How do you feel about it, now that it's a done deal?"

Sam smiled at Dee as she served him a cup of after-dinner coffee. "Thanks, Dee. How do I feel? Pretty damned strange, actually! Mixed feelings, of course. Guilt—related to my father. When I signed the final papers, I could have sworn I heard him, my grandfather, and my *great*-grandfather, all rolling over in their graves. But beyond the guilt, relief."

"Relief, Sam?" Dee looked at him curiously.

"Relief that I'll no longer have to sit listening to women spewing out their fury at men they once loved. Relief that I'll no longer have to sit listening to men telling me how great life's going to be once they've gotten rid of the "old bag"—not to mention worrying about all the kids I met, who'll forever bear the scars of all the vicious fighting they've had to witness."

He stirred sugar into his coffee. "But beyond the relief, a feeling of anticipation, a sense of...joy. And, I have to admit, more than a little trepidation. It's a totally new venture, and I don't know yet if I'm going to be able to hack it."

"You'll have Meg," James offered. "She could run that place with her eyes shut, couldn't she, Dee!"

"Oh, yes!" Dee hesitated a moment before saying to Sam, "I've talked to Meg several times on the phone since James and I got back. Andy's being very... difficult."

"You haven't talked to her at all, Sam, during this past month?" James took a sip of his coffee.

"No, I figured I'd give her and Andy a breathing space. Time to come to terms with having me in their lives. Losing you has been a loss, Dee, to both of them. They need to get used to not having you around. It's going to take a bit of adjusting."

"You'll go carefully, Sam?" James's tone was quiet.

"Yeah, I'll go carefully."

"I don't think you'll have any problem with Meg," Dee said. "Now that she understands why you never contacted her, all her resentment of you is gone. We always wondered, you know, why you'd acted so... cavalierly. I believed it was out of character for you. But Meg...well, being so much younger when you used to come to Seashore, she didn't know you as well as I did."

"My mother always claimed she idolized you,"

James murmured. "It must have been devastating to feel—the way she did—that you had betrayed her."

Sam's features tightened. "I have a lot to make up for. What I did to Meg was unforgivable—"

"Don't be too hard on yourself." James frowned. "The circumstances were—"

"Damn the circumstances!" With a sudden spurt of self-directed anger, Sam shoved back his chair. "Nothing can excuse what I did. I took advantage of an innocent girl and got her pregnant. If it takes me the rest of my life, I'm going to make amends."

A heavy silence fell over the small group. A silence that lingered...and killed the evening.

When they'd all finished their coffee, Sam got to his feet. "Thanks, Dee," he said, "for a terrific meal. It was great to see you both again, but I'll be on my way now."

His hosts walked him out to the car, and as he started the engine, Dee said, "Meg's not expecting you till tomorrow and I know she's going out tonight. Mark and Deb are throwing a big farewell party at the inn."

"Yeah, Mark told me, and that's one reason I'm going back a day earlier than planned. I'd like to be there—at least catch the end of it. I should be in Seashore by ten. If you should be talking to Meg, don't tell her I'm on my way." He set the car in motion. "I want to surprise her."

CHAPTER EIGHT

MARK put his arm around his fiancée's shoulders as he addressed all their friends who had gathered in the inn's cocktail lounge after a sumptuous buffet dinner.

"Most of you know," he said, "that Deb and I are going to be married in Chicago, because her mother's there—"

"She's in a nursing home," Deborah piped in, "and far too old and frail to travel—"

"So we're going to have our wedding at her bedside—and she's looking forward to it immensely!" said Mark.

Beaming, Deborah added, "Mom had almost given up hope of ever seeing her only daughter become a blushing bride!"

As everybody chuckled, Mark hoisted up the champagne flute in his hand. "Now, before we get down to the serious business of partying, I'd like to propose a toast." He looked over at Meg, who was at the back of the crowd. "To the inn's new Assistant Manager, Marguerite—" His gaze skipped beyond her, to the swing doors leading in from the foyer, and with a flash of his white teeth he raised his glass even higher. "And to her new boss, Sam Grainger!"

Meg's pulse froze...then it skittered forward. She hadn't expected Sam till tomorrow. As the toast was being drunk, she tensed, sensing his presence at her shoulder.

"Hi." His tone was low and slightly questioning, as if he wasn't sure what her reaction would be to his presence.

If he only knew! Her whole body *tingled* with awareness of him. She forced herself to ignore the starbursts of sensation dancing from nerve to excited nerve, and focus her mind on the decision she'd made during his absence.

The two of them, she'd reflected, were going to be thrown together by dint of his being the inn's new owner. They were also going to be thrown together by dint of his being Andy's father. She was well aware now that Sam was the kind of man who did *not* take his responsibilities lightly. She'd judged him in the past without knowing all the facts; and had treated him shamefully.

It was time for her to make a fresh start.

It was time to make amends...and there were two ways in which she could do that. Firstly, she could give him her wholehearted help in running the inn. And secondly, she could give him her wholehearted help in getting to know his son.

She could, and would, do both.

"Meg...?" He touched her elbow, gently.

She swallowed hard, and turned, slightly.

He was wearing jeans, and a navy crew-necked sweater over a finely checked flannel shirt. His hair was thick and longish and windblown; his jaw was shadowed, his breath minty, his green eyes fixed intently on her.

Dear God, if only he wasn't so attractive!

He did look tired...but the weariness in his features only served to make him more appealing to her. Her love for him overwhelmed her. She ached to caress the weariness away, ached to slide her arms around his lean waist, and—

"Hi," she said. And smiled. "Welcome home."

* * *

Sam punched his pillow, turned over onto his back, and stared up at the shadowy ceiling.

He still hadn't gotten over the shock of having Meg welcome him with so much warmth, so little reticence.

There had, of course, been *some* reticence.

He'd seen it in the wariness darkening her eyes, even as she smiled; he'd heard it in her faint in-hiss of breath when a waiter had bumped them together as they stood on the fringe of the crowd...

Making conversation.

"You've lost weight." He'd skimmed a concerned glance over her. Despite the demure cut of her black dress, the clinging silky fabric had revealed the too slender curve of her hips, the fragile span of her waist. "Dee tells me Andy's been giving you a hard time."

"You've seen Dee?"

"I stopped by for dinner on the way here. She said Andy's—"

"We have to give him time."

She'd spoken calmly but he'd seen the flutter of a pulse at the base of her throat. He could only guess at how hurtful it must be, having her son turn against her.

"What can I do?" he'd asked.

He thought he'd seen a sparkle of tears in her eyes, but then it was gone and he wondered if he'd just imagined it.

"Nothing," she said. "Just...be yourself when you're around him. That's all you can do."

"Are we OK?" he'd asked. "You and I?"

She didn't play dumb and he admired her for that.

"Yes." Her gaze was direct. "You and I are OK."

Mark had drifted over then and he'd gotten sidetracked. When he looked for Meg again sometime later, she'd gone. He'd felt a pang of disappointment; he'd wanted to talk with her some more...

Mark and Deborah were planning to stay that night at

Elsa's, before taking off next afternoon for Chicago. When the party was over, they escorted Sam to the owner's ground-floor suite, where they said their good-byes.

Sam had been tired, and after they'd departed he'd gone straight to bed...only to find he couldn't sleep. Couldn't sleep for thinking about Meg...

Now with his hands clasped behind his head, he lay listening to the rhythmic crash of the waves, and let his thoughts sift back to the night Andy had been conceived.

Meg had told him it happened under the arbutus tree, down below the inn. He frowned, concentrated, tried his level best to drag those memories from his deepest sub-conscious...but with no luck.

Damn, why couldn't he remember?

How could he forget? Forget having sex with some-one as sweet and as lovely and as desirable as Meg Stafford?

Guilt had him grimacing as he recalled that she'd just turned eighteen.

Oh, dammit to hell!

He lurched up from the bed and stumbled over to the window. The moon was full, the sea a glittering glory of pewter and jet. His eyes were drawn to that tree on the beach, the carpet of grass and wildflowers under its twisted branches lying now in the darkest of shadows.

Had it been shadowy that night?

Had it been—

He froze as he remembered something. Remembered how, when he'd held Meg in his arms the day Andy arrived back from camp, he'd had the oddest sense of déjà vu.

I've held her like this before, he'd thought. I've looked down into her face like this before, into those blue blue eyes before.

But he'd dismissed it—forgotten it, actually—when

Andy had burst into the kitchen and Meg had wrenched herself free.

Yes, the memories were in there somewhere, but he doubted the rest of them would ever come back. That night was lost and gone forever. But the fruits of it remained.

He pressed his hands against the cool windowpane and pressed his forehead there, too. He closed his eyes.

Meg had been only eighteen. Eighteen and—

Innocent?

He jerked his head from the glass and felt an icy chill skate over his naked body. Dear God, he'd never once thought about the implications of that word. He recalled using it in his conversation with Dee and James, when he'd told them he'd taken advantage of an innocent young girl—but he'd meant only that Meg had been naïve; unworldly. He groaned. *Had* she been innocent? *Truly* innocent? Had he stolen something from her that he could never return?

He clenched his right hand into a fist and pounded it savagely against the wall. Over and over and over again.

"Your father's back," Meg said to Andy when he came downstairs next morning. "He was at Mark's party."

Andy swung his pack over his shoulder and, avoiding her eyes, shuffled toward the back door. "Gotta go— I'm late."

"But you haven't eaten breakfast!"

"Not hungry."

"You'll have to start getting up earlier now that you can't walk to school!" Seashore wasn't big enough to justify having its own high school; local students were bused to Larch Grove, twenty miles away. "If you should ever miss the bus, how would you get to—"

"*Who cares!*" He slammed the door behind him.

Meg closed her eyes as the sound reverberated in her

head. The last month had been impossible. She'd tried every way she could think of to get through to Andy, but all her attempts had been blocked by his sullen defiance. Each morning by the time he left for school she had a roaring headache, and a knot in her stomach from the stress of trying to keep her temper.

Her hands shook as she poured cold water into a glass. She was *so* tired of making allowances for him—and, she decided determinedly as she downed a couple of aspirin, she wasn't going to put up with his rudeness any longer!

Tonight, come what may, she would deal with it.

"Good morning, Meg!" Katy, the new junior receptionist, smiled in greeting as Meg crossed the foyer on her arrival at the inn. A pretty redhead, Katy lived out by the golf course and drove to work in an old blue Honda. "Did you enjoy the party?"

"Yes, it was fun." A group of tourists crowded into the foyer and Meg glanced round briefly before returning her attention to Katy. "Is Mr. Grainger in his office?"

"In yours, actually!"

"Thanks." Meg crossed to her office, and after a light rat-tat on the door, went in.

Sam had been looking out the window; he turned as she entered. His back was to the light and for a second all she could see was his outline—tall, wide-shouldered, lean-hipped, long-legged. Powerful.

Then he stepped toward her and she saw he was wearing hip-hugging blue jeans and a denim shirt, the sleeves rolled casually up almost to the elbows. His gold watch glinted on his left wrist; on his forearms the dark hair curled in silky whorls. Sexy, sexy. She swallowed and dragging her gaze up, fixed it with a feeling of desperation on his face.

His eyes had never looked greener, or deeper—or, she thought with a feeling of panic, more seductive.

"Well, this is it, Meggie mine." His husky voice caressed her, stimulating thoughts that made her legs weak. He hitched a hip on the edge of her desk, and running a hand lightly through his jet-black hair, he tossed her one of his devastating trademark smiles. "I'm all yours."

Sam noticed Meg flush scarlet and could have kicked himself. He had embarrassed her—the very last thing he wanted to do.

But it was an awkward situation: their relationship, on the one hand, was professional...but because of the past, and Andy, it was also deeply personal.

"I could have worded that better—" he began, only to have her interrupt him with a perfunctory gesture.

"Don't worry about it." She hung her jacket on the coatrack and with brisk steps crossed to the file cabinet. Opening the top drawer, she riffled efficiently through a series of files and withdrew one. "Mark left this log for you." She gave it to him. "After you've read it through and assimilated it, if you've any questions, I'll try to answer them."

So...brisk and business-like was to be the order of the day—and *every* workday, he imagined. Fine, he could go along with that. It wouldn't be easy, though—she was just so damned beautiful. This morning her willowy figure was shown off to elegant perfection in a simple white sweater and tailored navy slacks; while her gamine hairstyle accentuated her fine bone structure and beautiful sky-blue eyes. Eyes that were staring at him levelly, demanding that he pay attention to...work.

He dropped his gaze to the log. "It'll take me a week or two," he murmured, "to get through all this stuff."

"In the meantime—" Meg rolled out her chair and sat down "—a busload of tourists has just arrived. Mark always made a point of greeting them personally before they went in to breakfast—perhaps you'd like to continue the tradition?''

He tucked the file under his arm and slid his hip off the desk. "Sure. What kind of spiel did he give them?"

"Oh, just that he was delighted they'd chosen the Seashore Inn, and if they required any information about the area, to take their questions to the front desk.''

He sketched a salute and as he passed her, managed not to roll his eyes in appreciation when he was treated to a drift of her seductive peachy perfume. "Will do."

The moment the door closed behind him, Meg sagged back in her chair. There, that hadn't been so bad. She'd gotten through their first minutes together as boss and employee and if they could continue as they'd started off, she could foresee no problems...

Other than the fact that just looking at him made her want to fling herself into his arms and kiss him. That smile alone, when he'd said "I'm all yours," had made her legs feel like melting butter—

With an effort she pushed him to the back of her mind, and set herself to tackling the pile of new mail in the in-basket and phone calls that had to be returned.

She was busy all day and didn't see Sam again, except in passing, till she was leaving for home after her shift. She'd gone round the back to get her bike when she noticed him approaching from the vacant adjoining property.

Her heart did its now-customary excited-flutter-thing, and her efforts to calm it were to no avail. Wheeling her bike quickly along the path toward the front, she sketched a vague wave in his direction and hastened on her way.

"Hang on a minute!" he called.

Meg paused. And tightened her grip on the handlebars.

"How was your day?" he asked as he drew close.

"Busy. How was yours?"

"Odd." His face creased in a smile. "I couldn't decide whether I felt more like a guest or a host or an inspector or a pest! A pest, I think!"

"You're the boss!" she said lightly. "Give it a week or two, it'll feel right."

"You're off home now?"

"Mmm. Andy's bus gets in around five." She knew, without checking her watch, that it was already after six. "I like to be there as soon after that as I can."

"How come you're still here then?"

"Deborah always stayed till six, so I've adopted her hours."

"Meg, you don't have to. We can change that, if—"

"I'll see how it works out," she said. "Now I'd better get going."

She made to push the bike forward but Sam stopped her by circling her left wrist with his long fingers.

"I'd like to see my son," he said quietly. "Would it be OK if I dropped by this evening?"

Her hesitation was almost imperceptible. And when she spoke, it was with a confidence in her tone that was totally at odds with her inner apprehension. How would Andy handle the visit? Would he treat Sam with the same unveiled antagonism she'd been suffering for the past month?

"Come by around eight," she said. "That'll give me time to get the kitchen cleaned up after dinner."

And time to have that talk with Andy that she'd promised herself.

After she'd put away the dinner dishes that evening, Meg was about to broach the subject of Andy's behavior with him when he scooped up his textbooks from the kitchen table where he'd been working and headed for the door to the hall.

She frowned. "Where are you going?"

He kept walking. "I've still got tons of homework to do and I'm going to finish it upstairs."

"Just a minute." She followed him across the room.

He turned and presented her with a stony look.

"I told you your father's coming. I want you here."

"Why?"

"You should get to know him."

"Why?"

"Because it's only fair."

"To who?" The surly insolence in his tone grated on Meg's nerves.

"To both of you." She could feel her temper rising.

"Look, you're the one who slept with him! I don't have to—"

Her temper finally exploded. It felt as if something in her head just snapped. She swung her arm up with every intention of slapping him...and only at the very last moment did she realize what she was doing and regain control of herself. She froze, her hand a mere two inches from his face, and her mouth opened in a gasp of dismay.

She had never, *ever* struck her child. She could hardly believe that she'd almost done it now!

Neither, apparently, could Andy.

As she dropped her hand, he stared at her, his eyes wide, his expression a mixture of shock and incredulity.

And then...he snorted. A jeering, sneering sound.

"Go on," he taunted. "Hit me. That's what you want to do, isn't it?"

"Andy." She reached out to him. "I'm sorry, I didn't mean to—I wouldn't have—"

He wrenched himself away from her. "It's all because of him! You'd never have done anything like that before *he* came along!'' He spun round and shouting, ''I *hate* him! And I hate you, too!'' he lurched out of the kitchen, his backpack thumping against the doorjamb as he went.

She heard him break into a run in the passage, heard the angry thud-thud of his feet as he stormed up the stairs.

She bit her lip so hard she almost pierced it.

Closing her eyes, she collapsed into the nearest chair and with her head in her arms on the table, gave in to the despair she felt over her unforgivable loss of control...

And over her painful inadequacy as a mother.

Sam knocked on the kitchen door but there was no reply.

He knocked again, more loudly this time.

He heard what sounded like a chair being scraped back, and then, after what seemed a very long time, the door was opened, and Meg appeared. Without a word, she stood back to let him in.

''Hi,'' he said. ''I'm sorry I'm so late but—''

He broke off and his brows knit in a dark frown as his gaze encompassed her. Her hair was damp and spiky, her eyes red-rimmed, her cheeks mottled and flushed.

He clamped his jaw grimly. ''Andy?''

From upstairs, came the sound of a crash.

Meg jumped.

''Get your jacket!'' Sam looked around, saw it draped over a chair. In one rough sweep of his hand he snatched it up and thrust it at her. ''You need to get out.''

''But...'' She glanced distraughtly upward.

''Leave him a note.'' His tone was terse.

''You don't understand, I've been—''

''Do it!''

He heard her inhale a deep rasping breath that seemed to come from the depths of her soul. But then she turned from him, searched in a drawer for pencil and pad, scribbled a note and propped it on the table, against the salt shaker.

"Right." He grabbed her hand. "Let's go."

"Where to?"

"To a little pub I know, halfway between here and Larch Grove. You and I," he said, "have to talk."

The Vine and Dine was situated on the banks of a river.

The cocktail lounge was dimly lit, but the mirrored bar was ashimmer with bottles and glasses. Sam guided Meg to a small table in an alcove overlooking an illuminated garden.

When the waitress came over, Sam ordered two brandies.

After she'd served the drinks and moved away, Sam said, "So...do you want to tell me what happened tonight? I assume you and Andy fought because he didn't want me coming over to the house."

Meg felt her heart twist as she recalled how badly she'd handled their confrontation. "He was angry...and he was...insolent." Her eyes slid from Sam's steady gaze and fixed on her hands, which were clutched together on the table in front of her. "I...came close to slapping him. I almost lost it...completely."

"Oh, Meg." He reached over and cupped her hands with his. "This has all been so hard on you..." His grip tightened. "Hard on you both."

Her tension started—magically—to unfurl, as she heard the caring in his voice. Till this moment, she hadn't quite realized she wasn't in this alone. Whatever happened, Sam would support her; of that she was sure.

She withdrew her hands from his and reached in her bag for a tissue. "It *is* a difficult time." Her voice still had a faint tremor. She blew her nose, returned the tissue to her purse. "For *all* of us...but especially for Andy."

Sam sat back in his chair. "Maybe if you told me a

bit about the past I'd be able to understand him better—get a fix on how to approach him. Since the divorce, his family has been you and Dee, with Elsa as a surrogate grandmother?''

''Yes.''

''When did you and Jack get married?''

''A couple of years after Andy was born.''

''Was he a local guy?''

''He lived in Larch Grove but worked as a mechanic at the gas station up by Matlock's Marina. Dee and I needed work done on the Volvo—that's how I got to know him.''

''Were you in love with him?''

''I think now,'' she said slowly, ''that I deceived myself—talked myself into believing I was in love. I guess what I really wanted was a dad for Andy, but—'' her tone held a faint thread of bitterness ''—it didn't work out that way.''

''Did Jack want children of his own?''

''No. And in the end, he blamed Andy for our breakup. He said he was too young to be tied down with a child.''

''How old was Andy when you divorced?''

''Seven.''

''Did he…get badly hurt?''

''By that time, he knew the score. He knew Jack had no interest in him.''

''And you had no clue, no hint, when you were going out together that he didn't like kids?''

''When Jack was courting me, he also set out to court Andy—and he succeeded. Andy absolutely adored him.'' Meg sipped from her glass but hardly tasted the brandy. ''If I'd had any doubts about accepting Jack's marriage proposal, Andy's love for him swept those doubts away.''

Even now, the memories of Jack's rejection of Andy

made her want to weep. "Once we settled down to married life, Jack's attitude to Andy changed. He stopped paying attention to him, and Andy obviously couldn't understand it. When he found his overtures constantly rebuffed...well, it was painful to see the light go out in his eyes."

She saw Sam's features tighten.

"So you see," she went on, "why Andy's not about to leap into a relationship with you. He's been burned once, badly burned."

"Poor kid." Sam toyed with the stem of his glass. "It's going to be an uphill battle, gaining his confidence."

"I'm afraid so."

Silence hung over them, and continued to linger. They finished their drinks, and after Sam settled the bill he escorted Meg from the lounge.

Outside, the air was sweet with the scent of honeysuckle. Down by the river, couples were strolling in the moonlight, on a path that ran along the reeded bank.

"Fancy a walk?" Sam asked.

Meg hesitated.

He took her hand, led her down the slope toward the path. Her fingers were warm, the bones elegant, her skin smooth as magnolia petals. He couldn't help comparing her hands with Alix's—they'd been elegant, too, but her palms had been tough; tough as the woman herself.

"Penny for them?" Meg's voice broke into his thoughts.

He tightened his clasp. "I was thinking about Alix."

"Do you...miss her?"

"I...miss what I *thought* we had." A group of laughing women swarmed by and crowded in front of them. He cupped Meg's elbow as they came to a fork in the path. "Let's get out of here," he muttered. "Up this way."

Gradually as they walked, the sounds of other humans faded away. The path they'd chosen ended up at a gazebo, its trellised structure white-frosted by the moon.

As the sound of their steps on the sunbaked path ceased, stillness fell over the place. A stillness that was absolute. Or so it seemed, in those first few seconds.

But gradually, as she listened, Meg could hear sounds. Crickets. Furtive scurryings in the grass. The hum of a flying insect. The distant hoot of an owl.

"What was it," she asked Sam, "that you *thought* you and Alix had?"

For a moment, she thought he wasn't going to reply. Then he said huskily, "I can't talk about it. Not…yet."

"I'm sorry—"

He waved her words away. "One thing I *do* know," he said. "I'll never marry again."

The cry of a bird came to them from down by the river. It had a lonesome sound.

"You've been burned, too," Meg said. "Just like Andy."

"How about you? At Dee's wedding you said 'Once was enough.' Did you mean that?"

"Yes. I'm very happy the way I am. And you only made one mistake…I made two—"

"You're counting me as the first, of course?"

"To be honest, yes, I *was* counting you. That was a mistake. I got carried away, by—"

"Compassion." He took her by the shoulders, made her look at him. "That's nothing to be ashamed of, Meg."

Compassion. What would he think if he knew she'd been carried away by much more than compassion!

"At any rate," she said, "I'll not marry again. I have my family, my job, my friends. What more could I want!"

You! The word shot into her mind with such intensity

that for a horrifying moment she thought she'd spoken it.

"So here we are," he murmured. "Sam Grainger and Meg Stafford, uncommitted and sworn to remain so. How would you feel, Meggie mine, about the two of us having an affair? No strings, no promises. Just two... lovers on the loose!"

An affair with Sam. Vivid images sprang unbidden to her mind: images that were Technicolor, exotic... x-rated. But even as a blush flooded her cheeks, she saw a twinkle in Sam's eyes, and realized he was having her on.

She also realized that for one heady, dangerous moment she'd been tempted to accept his offer. She was appalled to discover how frail her armor was against this man's charm.

But that was something *he* must never know!

So...somehow managing a light laugh, she answered him in a tone that was amused...and faintly mocking to boot.

"In your dreams, Sam Grainger. *In your dreams!*"

CHAPTER NINE

MEG stood in her driveway and watched the rear lights of Sam's Infiniti disappear along the street.

She hadn't invited him to come in.

"I want to talk to Andy," she'd explained. "And it would be better if—"

"If I'm not around. I understand. And Meg—" his expression was serious "—good luck."

She'd need it, she thought now as she turned and made her way to the back door...if Andy was still in the mood he'd been in when she left.

She found him in the sitting room, huddled deep in an armchair, but he didn't hear her come in as he had the TV on. Her eyelids flickered as she saw he was watching the news...and Alix Grainger.

Dark and vivacious—and oozing controlled urgency—Sam's ex-wife was standing in the foreground of a bombed street with a riot going on behind her. Her khaki shirt was stained, as were her khaki trousers. A fierce wind gusted her long hair across her cheeks, and as she talked into the camera, she used an impatient hand to hold the curling strands back from her eyes. Cat's eyes: topaz, tilted, sharply intelligent but guarded—

"How come their marriage broke up?"

Andy's voice made her start. She looked at him. His face was pale, and her heart went out to him when she saw the grimy evidence of tears on his cheeks. His tone had been brusque...but at least he was talking to her. "Sorry?"

"How come he's not married to her anymore?"

"I don't know."

"Didn't you *ask* him?"

"He doesn't want to talk about it."

"Now that he's broken up with *her*, is that why he's after *you*?"

"He's not after me, Andy. We're going to be running the inn together, so we need to get to know each other, in order to have a harmonious working relationship—"

"You weren't working tonight! You were out with him for more than two hours! What were you *doing*?"

"Just chatting." She gestured toward the TV. "Do you mind if I switch this off?" She lifted the remote control from the coffee table and clicked the Power button. Alix Grainger disappeared abruptly. "You and I have to talk."

"About what?" He scowled at her.

"About your attitude. I've given you a lot of leeway this past month because I know it's been hard for you, trying to adjust to the changes around here—but no more! From now on—no matter your mood or what you're thinking—I expect you to be polite. If you're not, I'll ground you."

He pushed himself up out of his chair. "Fine." He shrugged elaborately as if the matter were of no importance to him. "I'll be polite."

"To me...*and* your father?"

The pause was almost imperceptible before he said, "Sure. No problem." He opened his mouth wide in a noisy yawn that was blatantly fake, and started toward the door. "Good night," he said. "I'm off to bed now."

"About what happened earlier," she said quietly. "Andy, I truly am sorry."

He stopped in front of her and she realized, with a jolt of surprise, how tall he was. It wouldn't be long before he was as tall as she was. He was growing up. On his way to being a man. The thought brought with it a sense of impending loss that made her feel unbearably depressed.

"Don't worry about it," he said. But there was, in his eyes, a shuttered look she'd never seen there before. "It's over. Forgotten."

But she knew it wasn't forgotten. Would have known it even if he hadn't brushed by her without giving her his usual good-night hug, because his shuttered eyes had told their own story: polite he would be, but other than that, he would make no concessions.

It was clear that he was not about to accept his father. And as long as she and Sam Grainger continued their association, he was not about to accept her, either. He had drawn a line in the sand. He had put himself on one side; and his father on the other.

And she, who loved them both, was in the middle.

Next morning when she got up she knocked on Andy's door to waken him and then set off for her regular run, but the beach was shrouded in a white fog so she cut the run short.

When she got back, Andy was in the kitchen, putting his cereal plate and a glass into the dishwasher.

"Good morning," she said, and added, as he put on his jean jacket, "You're not leaving already, are you?"

"Yeah, I'm meeting Mike at the corner."

"You're early!"

"You gave me a hassle about being late yesterday." His tone was flat. "You going to give me a hassle now about being early?"

"No, it's just that—"

"Look, I've gotta go. I don't want to keep Mike waiting. OK?"

"Yes, of course."

He swung up his backpack. "See you tonight."

And then he was off. No smile. No goodbye hug.

He'd been polite enough, she had to give him that. She couldn't *force* him to be warm, friendly...himself.

Sighing, she went upstairs to shower and get dressed. Things would get better. All she had to do was wait, give him more time. But no matter how she tried to convince herself of that, she didn't succeed. Andy was stubborn. Always had been. Even as a small child, once he'd made up his mind to do something, nobody could budge him.

She'd never seen any sign that that had changed.

Her anxiety about him niggled at her as she got dressed; niggled as she drank her morning coffee; and *still* niggled as she rode her bike through the mist to the inn.

But when she walked into the lobby and saw Sam leaning against the reception desk, her worries about Andy were forgotten as she stared, besottedly, at his father.

He was wearing an exquisitely cut taupe suit with a crisp white shirt and a silk tie the same startling emerald as his eyes...

Those eyes, however, were fixed on Katy, who looked as dazzled as if she were staring into the sun.

Meg felt a piercing pang of jealousy—she who had always believed she didn't have a jealous bone in her body. Even as she reeled from it, she berated herself. She had no right to feel in any way possessive of Sam Grainger. He might be the father of her child, but he was, to use his own words, a "lover on the loose." Not committed to her, nor to any other woman. Not now, not ever.

She hailed the two with a casual "Good morning!" as she walked toward her office.

Katy smiled. "Good morning, Meg."

"Good morning," Sam said...and with an "Excuse me, Katy," followed Meg across the lobby. When she reached out to open her door, his hand got to the knob first.

"Allow me!" he murmured, and walked her into the room.

With her heartbeats tumbling over each other, she slipped off her jacket and hung it on the coatrack.

"How did it go last night," he asked, "with Andy?"

"We talked." Meg tucked her bag into the bottom drawer of her desk. "He's promised to be polite. To both of us."

"Well, I guess that's a step in the right direction." He shoved his hands into his trouser pockets; she heard the jingle of keys or coins. "Look, I've been thinking about Andy and how I should handle the situation..."

As she gazed at him, she felt the way Kate had looked: bedazzled. It was his eyes, of course; those mesmerizing green eyes. So very distracting. She made a supreme effort to listen to what he was saying but it was impossible to concentrate.

"...And I came to the conclusion," he went on, "that my best route would be to put absolutely no pressure on Andy to have him accept me. But at the same time, not allow him to dictate how you and I should relate to each other. Right?"

She murmured vaguely, ran the tip of her tongue over her lips, which suddenly felt dry.

"He knows you and I are going to be working together. But when he sees that you and I are not only colleagues but friends, my hope is that he'll eventually get used to my dropping by, used to us going out together. As friends do. So...what do you think?"

Meg had to scramble for an answer when he came up with the question. What had he said? Something about their being friends? But could they ever be that, considering the way she felt about him?

"Meg? What do you think? Do you agree?"

Think about...what? Agree to...what? She tried to look intelligent as she said, "Oh, yes, absolutely."

"Then here's the plan. I drop by your house frequently and we also go out together, socially, from time to time."

Oh, Lord...was *that* what she'd agreed to? Well, it served her right...she had only herself to blame, letting herself fall under his spell instead of *listening*.

She managed a croaky "OK."

"So how about I drop by this evening, just hang out?"

She finally got a hold of herself. "The dropping by is fine—"

"Terrific."

"—But as for the hanging out," she added smoothly, "sorry, no deal. I've a list a mile long of things that need doing. Tonight you can switch Dee's bedroom furniture with Andy's because he wants to move to the bigger room!"

"Will do," he said.

"Come by around eight—" The phone rang on her desk, and as she picked it up, he murmured "See you later then," and left her to deal with the call.

But though he closed her door behind him, her image stayed with him. She was looking terrific this morning in gray slacks and a silk shirt the same blue as her eyes...but while he'd talked to her about his plans for dealing with Andy, those eyes had become hazy. Her mind had wandered, that had been obvious. What had she been thinking? He knew what *he'd* been thinking! He'd been thinking he'd better get out of there fast before she noticed he'd become aroused! Heck, when she'd run the tip of her tongue over her lips, he'd had to suppress a caveman urge to lean over her desk and grab her and taste that moist raspberry-pink flesh—

And that, he decided wryly as he went into his office,

would have been one huge mistake. How could he and
Meg ever achieve a successful business relationship if
he started the day by kissing her silly!

Sliding his suit jacket over the back of his swivel
chair, he sat down and whirled the chair around so he
was facing out to the gardens. As his discomfort began
to ease, he determinedly erased Meg's image from his
mind and focused on work. And particularly on the problems that had to be dealt with regarding his newly ac-
quired property...

As Burton had warned him, Mark had let the place
run down. The inn's charm was undeniable, but it
couldn't stand close inspection. Under the surface was a
hint of shabbiness, which given another year or so,
would become more than a hint.

Renovations were in order. The question was, where
to begin?

Sam considered the exterior first. The roof was new;
and the siding had been repainted last year. The parking
area needed repaving, but that could wait till next spring.
Lighting above the side doors could be improved, and
that would be done soon. The front entrance lacked ramp
access for wheelchairs, and that should be rectified immediately.

As to the interior, many of the bedrooms needed re-
decorating; many of the bathrooms needed moderniz-
ing...

He swiveled round again and leaned over his desk;
planning, and jotting down notes. Making phone calls,
and writing out figures. Figures that made his head whirl.

He had lunch sent in at one; and hardly raised his
head from his task again till around six-thirty, when all
at once he realized he was starving.

Stretching, yawning, he shoved his chair back and got
to his feet. He would eat in the dining room, he decided,
and then get himself along to Meg's.

*   *   *

"Mom, I need help with this math."

Meg pulled a steaming peach pie from the oven and set it on the countertop. Tugging off her oven gloves, she crossed to Andy, who was hunched over the table.

"Oh, algebra." She winced when she saw he'd erased his work so often the page of his notebook was torn. "So…what don't you understand?"

"How do you *do* this? I can't get my answer to match the answer at the back of the book."

"Are you working out what's in the brackets first?"

"Huh?"

"Before you multiply by the number *outside* the brackets, you have to add and subtract all those fractions *inside* the brackets." She turned away and started emptying the dishwasher. "The rules are there in your textbook, Andy. You'll never get anywhere with algebra if you don't understand and learn the basics."

"Yeah…" But his tone was absent. And when she glanced at him, he was scribbling furiously.

She had just finished emptying the dishwasher when she heard him say, "Gotcha!"

"How many more do you have to do?"

"That's it." He shut the textbook and shoved it away.

"Go over the rules," she said firmly. "Learn them."

"*Now?*"

"This evening. I'll test you before you go to bed."

"Algebra! What use is algebra going to be to me?" he protested sulkily. "Tell me that, Mom!"

Before she could answer him, there was a sharp rat-tat on the back door.

"I'll get it!" Andy lurched to his feet. "It'll be Mike. He's got a new computer game he wants to show me." Snatching the excuse to leave his books, he hurried over to the door and swung it open.

Facing him, on the stoop, was his father.

He froze.

Meg controlled an automatic urge to smooth her hair and instead made a welcoming gesture. "Hi, Sam. Come on in."

Dark color seeped up into Andy's face. He mumbled something unintelligible, moved out of Sam's way, and then hovered, as if not sure what to do next. But as Sam moved through the doorway, Andy's friend Mike appeared behind him.

"Oh, hi, Mike," Meg said. "Come on in."

Mike Matlock was short and wiry with a shock of red hair. He and Andy had been friends since kindergarten.

"Mike," Meg said, "this is Mr. Grainger—he's the new owner of the Seashore Inn." She guessed by Mike's swift glance at Andy that Andy had told Mike about Sam being his father. "Sam this is Mike Matlock. You may have met his parents at some time—they own the marina."

"Yeah," Sam said. "James and I went fishing with them a few times—way back when. Hi, Andy, nice to meet you."

Mike shook Sam's outstretched hand. "Hi, Mr. Grainger. My dad said he remembered taking you out on *Windstar*, and he said if I saw you I was to tell you you're welcome to take the boat out anytime."

"Thanks, I'll take him up on that offer. Hey—" he looked around "—how about if the four of us go out fishing?"

Andy scowled, but before he could object, Meg said quickly, "Let's do that, the first fine Saturday. Mike, will you check with your dad that that'll be OK with him?"

"Sure."

"Mom." Andy was barely managing to keep the resentment from his tone. "Is it OK if I go out with Mike for a while?"

Meg frowned. "I thought Mike was going to show you his new computer game?"

"We can do that another time." Andy started toward the door, with Mike trailing behind him.

"Son." Sam's voice was casual. "Your mom wants me to move your bedroom furniture into your aunt Dee's old room. I'd appreciate if you could give me a hand, before you go out. And you can show me where you want everything placed."

For the longest moment, Andy didn't answer. He stood, with his hand on the doorknob, his face turned toward the door. Meg sensed the battle going on inside him. He had promised to be polite—and knew the consequences if he was not. Poor Andy; he was usually willing to oblige, but right now, the last place he wanted to be was with his father.

Finally, she saw him square his shoulders. "Sure." He swung round and without looking at Sam, made for the door to the corridor. "Come on, Mike."

They slouched out of the kitchen, and Meg exhaled the deep breath she hadn't even known she was holding.

"Hang in there, Meg." Sam touched her arm reassuringly in passing. "It's going to be all right. Be patient."

She managed a tight smile, and managed to keep it in place till he was out of the room. But as she heard his heavy tread fade along the corridor, she let her tight self-control give way, and she sagged, feeling limp as a wet rag.

It almost broke her heart to see the two of them so much at odds. Her son...and his father.

She loved them both, so very much.

But what was it going to take, for Andy to accept Sam as his dad? She began to despair if he ever would.

"Where do you want it?" Sam asked, as he and Mike carted Andy's oak computer table into Dee's room. "By the window?''

''To the left of the window, at an angle.'' Andy was right behind them, carrying his printer.

''OK.'' After the table was in place, Sam said, ''Right, let's get the computer.''

When they'd finished moving everything, Sam stepped back and looked around the bedroom.

''This is pretty nice,'' he said. ''You have a lot more space here. What's your mom planning to do with your room?''

Andy's gaze was fixed on the computer. ''A guest room, for Dee and James.'' He turned to Mike. ''Ready to go?''

''Sure.''

The two boys walked to the door, but as they reached it, Andy hesitated.

He turned, and for the first time all evening, looked straight into Sam's eyes.

''Thanks.'' The word came out stiltedly.

Sam felt an aching lump in his throat. His son looked so lonely, so...unhappy. What would the boy do if he were to walk over to him now and envelop him in a massive bear hug?

Punch him, no doubt.

''No problem,'' Sam said. ''See you guys later.''

After they'd gone, he wandered back to Andy's vacated bedroom. And found himself drawn to the picture wall.

He stood, with his hands in his trouser pockets, for a very long time, his gaze going from one photo to another, drinking in the record of his son's sporting successes, from the time he was knee-high to a grasshopper.

He brushed his forearm over his eyes when he finished his inspection. Damn, it was hard—it was almost unbearably hard, to know how much he had missed.

He swallowed back the raw lump in his throat, and left the room, shutting the door behind him.

When he went back to the kitchen, he found Meg had made hot chocolate. She was sitting at the table, sipping hers.

"What were you doing?" she asked as he paused in the doorway.

"Looking at the picture wall."

"Remember the night of Elsa's barbecue, when Dee said she'd like to get you settled in here...and I rushed over first to get Andy's room ready? I wanted to take down all the pictures where I thought he looked like you."

"I sensed something was up—but of course, I never imagined..." He leaned sideways against the doorjamb. "I'd like to see those pictures. And do you have any others of Andy? I know I can never go back and capture the past, but maybe I could get a sense of him, of him growing up, if I could live it through his photos."

"Oh, I've got loads of albums. They're all up in my room. After you have your cocoa, I'll take you up there and leave you to go through them."

Andy stayed out till close to ten.

He'd hoped his father would be gone, but as he cycled up the driveway, he saw that the Infiniti was still there. He got off his bike and reluctantly stopped to look at it. It was some car. He had to admit it.

But only to himself.

On their way out, Mike had drooled over it. He himself had tried to be cool.

"Oh, it's OK. But don't you think a Porsche is better? Or a Corvette? Yeah, if I had his kind of money—" He'd adopted a sneering tone. "I'd buy me a Corvette."

"Your dad...seems OK to me, Andy."

"Well it's not *your* mom he's after!"

As he recalled his fierce retort, Andy felt his anger rekindle.

He glared at the house as he walked his bike up past the car. His mom's bedroom light was on. None of the other lights were. His anger segued into something darker.

Parking his bike around the back, he opened the kitchen door and slipped noiselessly inside. He stood for a moment, and the only sound he could hear was the click-click-click of the clock on the stove.

Leaving his shoes by the door, he made his way stealthily along the darkened corridor, and up the stairs. The landing was unlit, but from his mother's bedroom door, which was slightly ajar, slanted a yellow beam of light.

His heart was thudding so hard he could hardly breathe.

What were they doing in there?

Silent as a stalking cat, he crept toward the door. He was almost there when he heard what sounded like a soft laugh. His smouldering anger—anger and jealousy and fear—all melded together till he couldn't control himself.

He lunged at the door, crashed it open.

And stormed into the room.

"What the...?" Sam jerked his gaze up from the album he'd been perusing, and stared at Andy. The boy had come to an abrupt stop halfway into the bedroom, his hands clenched into fists. His face was scarlet and contorted with emotion. His eyes were wild as they darted around.

"Where is she?" he demanded.

Sam closed the album and placed it on the bed alongside all the others spread out there—some open at pictures of Andy that he'd found particularly endearing or funny. He got up from the old rocking chair where he'd been sitting, and rounded the bed.

"Your Mom?" he asked quietly. "She's next door at Elsa's. Took a pie over, I think. What's wrong, Andy?"

Andy's gaze went past him; and jumped from one photo album to the next. Sam saw his Adam's apple bob up and down.

"You were...just looking at... I thought you and Mom were..." His voice trailed away, into silence.

He must have seen the light and thought they were both up here. His mother...and his father. And doing what? Sam didn't need much imagination to guess what Andy had been thinking. He felt a surge of compassion.

"No," he said. "Your mom just took me up here because she keeps her albums in her bedroom closet. I had asked if I could see pictures of you, growing up."

Andy folded his arms across his chest. "Why would you want to do that?" His belligerent expression was belied by the faint tremor in his voice.

"I missed out on all these years," Sam said. "The best I can do now is to look at the old pictures, imagine how it might have been, had I been a part of your life since the moment you were born." His smile was wry. "It's not much," he added, "but hey, it's all I've got."

Andy looked away from him, but Sam thought there was a sheen in his eyes that hadn't been there a moment ago.

"Andy—"

But the boy wheeled away. "I've got to do some algebra," he said, his voice muffled. "Before I go to bed."

A moment later, he heard Andy's bedroom door shut.

And right after that, he heard noises downstairs, and knew Meg had come back.

After putting the albums away he went downstairs, and met Meg in the front hall.

"Is Andy in?" she said anxiously.

"Yeah, he's back."

She breathed out a sigh. "Good."

He hesitated. Should he tell her what had transpired between him and the boy? No, he decided, best not. It would only upset her, and she had enough worries already.

"I'll be off now," he said. "See you tomorrow."

The sweet smell of baked fruit hung in the air, along with the seductively feminine scent from her skin and her hair. She was wearing a crew-necked white sweater and blue jeans, and she looked so beautiful he could have stood there all night, just looking at her.

"Sam?"

"Uh...yeah?"

Her smile took his breath away. "I'm looking forward to that outing on the boat."

"Yeah." He smiled back at her. "Yeah, so am I."

CHAPTER TEN

BUT next morning the weather changed.

A storm swept in from the west, bringing thunder, lightning, and curtains of lashing rain; and to Meg's disappointment, the *Windstar* outing had to be postponed.

The days that followed were equally wet, with gale-force winds that tore the remaining leaves from the trees, and whipped the ocean into a seething white-capped cauldron.

And after three weeks of the same relentlessly foul weather, Meg began to despair of ever seeing sunshine again.

At the inn, business had slacked off dramatically but she was kept busy helping Sam supervise the interior renovations he'd set in place, and during the day the place was a madhouse, with workmen coming and going, bearing ladders and carpets and paint pots and tools.

The bedrooms were scheduled to be finished on the last Monday of October, and late that afternoon, as she was tidying her desk, Sam poked his head into her office.

"Join me in the grand tour," he invited, "before you go home."

He was wearing black cords and a black turtleneck sweater, and he exuded a faintly dangerous aura. An aura that set alarm bells ringing in her head. Inspecting bedrooms with this man, she decided, was *not* a good idea...

"Sure," she said.

He was, after all, the boss!

But by the time they reached the final point of their tour, which happened to be the honeymoon suite, she was sorely regretting her decision. Every sensual cell in

150

her body was afire for him and she was dizzy with long-ing...while *his* attention seemed focused completely on the new decor.

"So, Meggie—" he wandered across the reception area and into the bedroom "—what do you think?"

Following him, she wrenched her gaze from his wide shoulders and determinedly fixed it on the Laura Ashley wallpaper. "Very pretty." Her eyes flicked to the brass and white iron bedstead with its puffy white pillows and luxurious comforter. How wonderful, she mused dream-ily, to sink down on that bed on one's wedding night, with—

She jerked her thoughts from the seductive image and moved with quick steps to the window. A stiff wind was making the panes tremble. Just the way her heart was trembling. She looked out but could see nothing but black, save for the rear lights of a departing car.

The hair at her nape pricked as Sam came up behind her. Wrapping her arms around herself, she said brightly, "We never did get our sail." She kept her gaze fixed on the red rear lights gradually fading into the murky night.

"The forecast's great for the weekend. Want to plan for Saturday, the four of us, if we can get the boat?"

Sam had spent much of his free time at their house over the past few weeks, but Andy had shown no signs of thawing. He still treated his father with cool polite-ness—although Meg had once or twice seen him sneak secret looks Sam's way; assessing looks, wary looks...looks that exposed a tender vulnerability that caught at her heart. The child had obviously erected a wall between himself and his father, to protect himself from hurt. Though one part of him might desperately want to break that wall down, the other part, the fearful untrusting part, wasn't prepared to do so.

"Meg?" Sam prodded.

"Mmm." She kept her tone light. "Yes, great."

"Will you have to twist Andy's arm?"

"He'll be OK...as long as Mike's coming with us."

He made no reply, and she knew it wasn't the answer he'd have liked. But there was no point in building up his hopes; Andy was as stubborn as he'd always been.

She turned and looked up at him with apology in her eyes. "Sam...he has no idea he's hurting you."

"Of course he doesn't, Meg. Kids that age are very self-absorbed. He's taking his time, he wants to be sure he can count on me, before he makes his move. But he will make that move. I'd bet my life on it."

"I hope you're right." She sighed. "I just wish I could do something..."

"There's nothing either of us can do, except go on the way we're doing. He'll see, eventually, that he has nothing to fear from me. He'll see that he *can* trust me. I'm not going to let him down, Meggie. I'm not going to let either of you down. Ever again."

Her emotions were already fragile; now as she heard the sincerity ringing in his tone, tears sprang to her eyes. As one brimmed over, he wiped it away gently, with a fingertip. She felt her throat tighten. "I know. I do trust you, Sam."

Trust you...and love you.

The words ached to be heard but she didn't say them. He didn't want her love; didn't want any woman's love...

But he did want to kiss her; she could read it in the clouding of his gaze; the quickening of his breath.

She mustn't let him! She was far too weak, where he was concerned...and that bed...oh, it was far too close...far too tempting. She had to leave, before she did something she'd regret.

She cleared her throat but still, when she spoke, the words came out with a fuzzy edge. "I should go."

Sidestepping him, she made for the door. "I have to get home."

Her heart gave a panicky flutter as he followed her.

"Meg!" His tone was urgent.

She kept walking. "I'll talk to Andy about Saturday." She made her tone brisk, hoping he'd get the message that she wasn't interested in...dallying. "After you check that we can get the boat."

He fell into step beside her as they walked along the corridor to the elevator. Don't touch me, she begged silently. Don't even put one finger on me or I'll fall into your arms and—

"Do you fancy going to the Vine and Dine for a while this evening?" he asked.

He'd taken her there several times during the past few weeks. They'd been pleasant evenings...on the surface...but she'd been finding them increasingly stressful lately as she battled to hide her feelings from him.

"Thanks, Sam, but...er...Elsa's coming over. Dee sent me photos and Elsa wants to see them."

Dead silence. Her cheeks flushed. He must know she was deliberately putting him off. How long did it take, after all, to show someone a batch of photos!

He didn't respond till they were down in the lobby.

And when he spoke, it was lightly. "It might be a good idea," he said, "if I don't come around to your place again till Saturday. Give the kid a break from his old man. You know what they say...absence makes the heart grow fonder!"

He'd spoken lightly...but the lightness, she sensed, had been forced. Andy had rejected him...now she would seem to be rejecting him, too. Why was this all so *difficult*?

"That might be a good idea," she replied.

He walked her over to her office door.

"So…" She paused in the open doorway. "We'll leave it till Saturday?"

His smile was tight. "Saturday it is!" He strode off in the direction of the dining room.

Guilt stabbed Meg as she entered her office. Was she being unfair, depriving Sam of the chance to see Andy just because she was afraid to spend time with him herself? Yes, it was unfair…but she had to protect her own heart. The more she saw of Sam, the more deeply she loved him. One of these days, if she didn't watch out, she would give herself away…and that would put her in an untenable position.

Sam called the marina that evening and talked with Mike's father. After the preliminary greetings, Sam brought up the proposed outing and asked Dave if he could use *Windstar* on Saturday, weather permitting. He was assured he could.

"So how are things working out at the inn?" Dave asked.

"Terrific, so far. Couldn't have done it without Meg, of course. She's been wonderful."

After a pause, Dave said, hesitantly, "Is it true what Mike tells me, Sam? You're Andy's father?"

"It's true, all right."

"Isn't that something? Heck, I thought it was just some unfounded rumor—I have to tell you the town's humming with it, Sam. You know the way small towns are."

Dave Matlock was mayor of Seashore and highly respected; it would be a good thing, Sam decided, to tell him the facts and enlist his help in getting the truth out so the story didn't get twisted and reflect badly on Meg.

"Dave, you remember when Alix was reported killed thirteen years ago in that helicopter explosion?" He went on to tell the other man the bare bones of what had happened afterward, and finished by saying, "I'm divorced now, but there's inevitably going to be a lot of talk, and—"

"Don't worry, I'll make sure everybody knows the truth. I have a lot of friends here, I'll enlist their help in squelching any nasty gossip. By the way...how's Andy taking the news? I've noticed he's not himself lately."

"You're right...but I'm hoping he'll come around."

"That stepfather of his—well, Andy had a tough start and deserves a break. He's one real good kid."

"Yeah, that's for sure."

After they hung up, Sam prowled restlessly around the office. So...word had already gotten around town about his being Andy's father; and it wouldn't require the brains of an Einstein to figure out that he'd been married to Alix at the time of Andy's conception.

How long would it be before word spread outward...first to Larch Grove, then farther...

How long before the media picked up the story? Oh, not because of him; by himself he wasn't newsworthy...but because of Alix, who was known the world around.

Dammit, he had to tell her. Warn her. Prepare her.

He didn't *want* to talk to her. But he had no choice.

He crossed to his swivel chair and dropped down into it. Then gritting his teeth, he reached across the desk and plucked the black phone from its cradle.

For Meg, the week dragged...because of Sam.

He seemed different—detached—since the night she'd rejected his invitation to go to the Vine and Dine. When they had occasion to talk, she got the feeling he wasn't quite with her.

Even when he'd told her that *Windstar* was available on Saturday, his mind had seemed elsewhere. She was *not* looking forward to the outing. It was going to be miserable, what with Andy being cool to Sam, and Sam being cool to her!

When Friday rolled around and Sam's brooding mood hadn't lifted, Meg decided to do something about it. She made up her mind to talk with him before going home, try to get things back on their previous friendly footing. But when she walked through to his office at six, all keyed up to broach the subject with him, the room was empty.

She went from there to the front desk. "Katy…"

Katy glanced up from a ledger. "Yes, Meg?"

"I'm looking for Mr. Grainger. Have you seen him?"

"He's gone—he had to pick up a part for his car, in Larch Grove. He stopped by on his way out, asked me to page him right away if any calls should come in for him."

Meg made an impatient tsking sound. "Thanks, Katy." She turned to go, but the receptionist called after her.

"I'm going to the movies tonight. Want to come? It's that new Meg Ryan comedy, supposed to be *really* funny!"

About to beg off, Meg impulsively changed her mind. At least it would be a couple of hours of mindless escapism; perhaps she'd even get a few chuckles. "I'd like that."

"It starts at seven—I'll meet you outside the Rialto at ten to."

As Meg cycled home, she tried to cheer up, but was unable to overcome her disappointment at having missed Sam. She'd so badly wanted to clear the air before their outing. And there was no point in waiting till they were on the boat; there'd be no chance to speak privately with the boys there.

But…she could come back to the inn tonight after the

movie! Katy would have the car, she'd ask her to drive her to the inn and drop her off.

Meg felt her spirits rise as she mulled over the idea. Yes, she decided, that's what she'd do. It would be well after nine by then, and Sam would surely be home.

Why the *devil* hadn't Alix returned his call?

Sam paced frustratedly around his suite, going from the sitting room to his bedroom, and then back to the sitting room again, with a detour each time through the den.

He'd phoned her agent on Tuesday night, and on learning she was due back in the country within the next twenty-four hours, he'd left a message asking that she call him at the inn immediately she returned. Now it was Friday evening, and he'd still heard nothing! What was—

The phone on the coffee table shrilled and he leaped for it. "Grainger!" He held his breath...and waited.

Five heartbeats later, he heard her voice—that familiar alto, husky and vibrant. "Sam, it's me. Alix—"

"Well *finally*! Where the hell are you?"

"And hi to you, too! I'm in a 7-Eleven in a little hick town called—" Another pause, a muffled, *What's this place called?* Then her voice came to him again. "Larch Grove."

"What?"

"I flew to Seattle, rented a car. Sam, I'm on my way. Just tell me how I get to the inn once I reach Seashore."

Huddled into her jacket, Meg walked around the side of the inn, having decided not to approach Sam's suite through the front lobby in case any of the staff wondered why she was visiting the boss after-hours.

When she rounded the corner, she found the back of the inn in darkness, save for a long yellow strip slanting

onto the path from Sam's sitting room window, and farther along, one lone lamp glowing above the entrance
door.

As she neared the sitting room window, she heard a
woman's voice, and at the same moment, realized his
window was ajar. She tensed and her heart gave a painful twist; it had never occurred to her that he might have
company.

Biting her lip, she made to turn away...but even as
she did, she recognized the voice. It was Alix Grainger's.

She started—then gave a dry chuckle and felt her tension ease. She'd been mistaken in thinking Sam had a
woman with him; he was just watching the TV news...

Taking in a deep breath, she resumed walking, the
soles of her runners making no sound on the path. The
reporter's voice continued on, and as Meg passed the
window, she snuck a look inside, unable to resist a secret
peek at Sam as he—

Her heart slammed against her throat.

Sam was not alone. Alix Grainger was there, with
him, in his sitting room. No voice from afar, no image
on a screen. Alix Grainger, in the flesh...

And in Sam's arms. With her head flung back, her
gaze confident, her body arched intimately against his.
She looked stunning with her long ebony hair curling
down her back, her voluptuous figure attired in a flame-
red sweater dress that skimmed provocatively over every
curve—

Meg grasped the entire scene in a mind-spinning frac-
tion of a second before she flung herself sideways, out
of the light. Panting, she fell weakly against the wall.

Words, phrases, drifted to her ''...Lois's cabin...I
know you'd...then...your message, asking me to call
you...as soon as...''

Sam had phoned Alix.

He had summoned her.

And she had come running.

Meg shuddered. She didn't want to hear more. She'd move in a minute, when her heartbeats came unjammed and her legs stopped their awful shaking—

"...Broke up because we didn't have a child...but now that you have a son, darling...all that has *changed*!" Alix's voice was charged with excitement. "It's wonderful—I can't wait to meet him—we'll be a family—"

Horror exploded in Meg's head with such force she thought her brain might shatter. Lurching from the wall, she pressed a hand to her mouth to keep back a surge of bile. Somehow managing to place one foot in front of the other, she stumbled back along the path and made her way around to the front of the inn, and onto the beach road.

Later, after she was home, she remembered nothing of how she got there. She didn't know if she'd walked, or run...or crawled. But as she lay still and stark on top of her bed, she recalled in vivid detail every single sight and sound that had impinged on her from Sam's sitting room.

Only as dawn broke and she sat curled up on her window seat with swollen eyes and dry tear tracks on her cheeks, did she try to think the situation over logically.

But no matter how she tried to persuade herself that things weren't as black as they appeared, she couldn't forget what she'd heard: Sam and Alix's marriage had broken up solely because they hadn't had a child.

If that was the truth, and if Alix was as keen as she'd sounded to accept Andy, what was to stop the two of them getting married again...and gradually easing Andy into their lives...and by doing so, easing him out of her own.

Dread overwhelmed her at the thought of seeing Sam

again. How would he broach the subject with her? She knew him well enough now to know he wouldn't be unkind. At least, not deliberately...

But he had no idea she was in love with him.

"You shouldn't have come, Alix." Sam watched soberly as his ex-wife paced the sitting room, her long fingers thrusting with repeated agitated movements through her ebony hair. "The fact that I have a child makes no difference to—"

"Oh, I know that *now*!" She whirled to face him, a self-derisive laugh catching in her throat. "But when my agent finally tracked me down at Lois's cabin and said you'd left an urgent call for me—and this barely five minutes after reporters had turned up on the doorstep with a story about your having just found out you had a son twelve years ago, with another woman—well, I put two and two together—"

"And came up with entirely the wrong number. I merely wanted to warn you of what might be ahead. Apparently, I was too late." Sam crossed to the built-in bar area. "We both need a drink. What'll it be? Your usual?"

Alix's mouth twisted in a thin smile. "Knowing how you feel about drinking and driving, am I to assume you're not kicking me out right away?"

Ignoring her comment, he poured two Scotches, neat for her, with a splash of soda added to his own, and then walked over and served her drink.

She raised her glass. "To old friends."

Sam saw the faintly mocking glint in her eyes...but he also heard—or thought he heard—a ring of regret in that famous husky voice. He paused, drink in hand. The end of their marriage had been ugly and bitter and Alix had never shown one whit of remorse for what she'd done. Did she now, when it was aeons too late, wish she could undo—

"Sam." She waved her glass in front of his face and when he brought his gaze to focus on her again, he saw not one whit of vulnerability. He must have imagined it. Her eyes were brilliant with self-confidence, her smile more dazzling than he'd ever seen it, as she repeated the toast.

He forced a smile. "To old friends." He clinked his glass to hers, and took a sip of his drink while Alix tossed hers off in one go, her gaze challenging.

"You always could drink me under the table," he said. She spent much of her time in the company of men; she drank like a man.

She sank down into one of the low armchairs, and reached the empty glass up to him. "Refill?" She crossed her elegant legs and he caught a glimpse of crimson lace under the hem of her short dress.

She really was incredibly, voluptuously beautiful. But even as Sam noted the fact dispassionately, her image was superimposed by another image—one of Meg. Meg dressed in yellow, sitting on an ottoman, raising her hand to accept a mug of coffee. Meg. Sweet, and lovely, and warm...

He hadn't been able to keep his eyes off her that evening. And he remembered how, each time their eyes had met, he'd seen a shadow darken her expression. And when it had, it had darkened something inside him too. He hadn't been able to figure out why that should be—

"*Sam?*" Alix was staring at him curiously.

He shook his head. "Sorry..." Taking her glass, he refilled it and returned it to her.

She wrapped her fingers around the heavy crystal, and regarded him with those shrewd cat's eyes. He didn't look away, but he felt as if she was stripping his soul bare.

"There's someone else," she said slowly. "Isn't there?"

He looked at her blankly.

"My God," she said, "you're in love. Who is she, Sam?" Alix gulped down the second drink the same way she'd tossed off the first. "Is it the mother of your boy? This...Meg?"

In *love*? With *Meg*? Sam's mind reeled. Surely not! He'd sworn never to give his heart again, sworn never to—

"Oh, Sam. You're in love...and you don't even know it!" Face pale, Alix rose abruptly. "Men are so damned stupid." She set her glass on the mantelpiece and stood with her back to him for a moment. He thought her shoulders slumped slightly, then she squared them and turned round. She ran a hand through her hair, and he thought the gesture was weary. "Look, I'm tired. It's been a long day. Can you give me a room for the night? I'll be out of here at dawn, out of your way—"

His mind was still whirling, trying to cope with all the ramifications of what Alix had said. That he was in love. He just couldn't seem to get his thoughts in order.

"You can sleep here," he said abstractedly. "Take my room, I'll use that." He gestured toward the sofa bed.

"No, I won't sleep here." There was a coldness to her tone that hadn't been there before. "You may not want me, Sam, but I—" She broke off and then went on steadily, "Take me out to the front desk, get me a room."

It was, of course, the best solution.

He escorted her to the front desk, got her a key, and took her up in the elevator to the second floor. When they reached her room, she slipped the key into the lock, and opened the door.

"Let's say goodbye here, Sam."

"Alix—"

She put her hand on his arm. "We were all wrong for each other," she said softly. "You're home and hearth and family. I'm excitement, thrills, and change. What attracted us to each other in the beginning were our differences—but in the end, they were the very things that drove us apart. Go after her, Sam. Don't let what happened between us sour the rest of your life."

She rose on her tiptoes and brushed a light kiss across his cheek. "I'm glad I came. I think that now we can, both of us, lay the past to rest."

A heavy mist hazed the ocean on Saturday morning, but by ten o'clock, when Meg and Andy arrived at the marina, the sun had burned it all away, and the ocean sparkled invitingly.

The sunshine did nothing, however, to brighten Andy's bad mood.

"This trip's going to be the pits without Mike!" he grumbled as he trailed along the jetty at Meg's heels.

"I'm sorry he couldn't make it." Meg took off her long-sleeved shirt and after tucking her pink tank top into her shorts, looped the white shirt around her waist and knotted it in front. "It's too bad he's not feeling well."

"I wanted to spend the day at his place." Andy sent a moody gaze toward *Windstar*, which was bobbing at the far end of the jetty. "How come I couldn't?"

Meg saw Sam jump off the boat and as he strode toward them, she felt an odd tightness in her chest... along with a renewed sense of relief that Alix wasn't coming on the trip.

She'd discovered that only minutes before.

Earlier in the week, Sam had offered to pick her and Andy up this morning and drive them to the marina, but Andy had had a nine o'clock hockey practice scheduled at the rec center across the street from the marina, so she'd told Sam they'd meet him on the boat. And after the practice, when Andy had been storing his hockey gear in the marina office, she'd seen Sam walk along the jetty to the boat. Alone.

She'd heaved a grateful sigh. At least she didn't have to face his ex-wife this morning. Bad enough that she had to face Sam, knowing what she now knew—

"Mom!" Andy's voice was impatient, resentful. "How come I couldn't spend the day with Mike?"

"Because I want you with me. I've hardly seen you lately—you've been so busy since you started high school and I've been so tied up at the inn since my promotion."

"If you wanted to see me so badly, why couldn't we have done something *together*, then!"

"That's what we're doing now!" Her gaze was fixed on Sam. Casually dressed in a taupe sports shirt and jeans, he was smiling broadly as he approached. He looked happy, happier than she'd ever seen him. The knowledge only added to her own feelings of misery.

"I meant just *us*!" Andy said. "Like it used to be."

It would never again be the way it "used to be." But wouldn't Andy be surprised if he knew she shared his wish? "We *will* spend time together, but you also need to spend time with your father, so you can get to know each other."

She heard Andy muttering under his breath, and she forced her lips into a smile as Sam swung up to them.

"Ahoy there," he greeted them. "Isn't it a terrific day?" He glanced at Andy. "But I'm sorry Mike's sick. We'll have to do something to make it up to him once he's better." He turned his attention back to Meg and the thought came to her, as she saw the sparkle in his eyes, that he looked like the cat who had caught the

proverbial canary. She wanted to ask him where the canary had spent the night: in his bed?

Where else!

He frowned. "You look a bit washed out, Meg. You
OK?"

Washed out. Oh, yes, she'd look washed out...to him.
Who wouldn't, in comparison to the splendiferous Alix
Grainger! "I'm fine. Stayed up late watching TV." *Liar!*

He took her arm and ushered her along the jetty. The
swaying motion made her feel dizzy. Or...was it his
touch?

"You'll soon get some roses in your cheeks," he re-
assured her, "once we're out at sea."

· But she knew, only too well, that though the breeze
might indeed blow red roses onto her cheeks, it would
take a lot more than a few flowers to cure what ailed
her.

As the boat skimmed over the choppy waves, Sam sat
in the cockpit, savoring the warmth of the sun. And savoring the sight of Meg, who was taking a turn at the
wheel.

Even in an old pink tank top, shorts, tennis shoes and
a bulky orange life jacket, she was *incredibly* elegant.
Was the elegance in the litheness of her tall figure...or
was it in the graceful way she moved? He didn't
know...but what he *did* know was that just looking at
her gave him the same surge of pleasure he felt when
he looked at a field of wildflowers or a child's happy
face.

He glanced round at Andy, who was sitting across
from him. *His* face, unfortunately, wasn't happy! As he
glowered down at the ocean, only his profile was in
view, but there was no mistaking the sullenness of the
down-tilted mouth.

"Hey, Andy!" When he had the boy's attention, Sam

gestured toward a heavy rope lying on the deck. "Coil that up and tidy it away, would you, before somebody trips?"

"Yeah. In a minute."

Sam nodded, and turned to Meg again.

He noticed her arms were pink. Getting up, he ran a testing palm over her bare shoulder. It felt hot. "Are you wearing sunscreen?"

"Of course." She added, "I brought a shirt—I'll put it on shortly."

She'd started at his touch but hadn't shrugged his hand away. It felt good, to have his fingers on her skin, to feel it, smooth as expensive silk, under his own. She'd turned her face to him as she spoke; her gaze was steady...and oddly challenging.

He ran his fingers around her neck. "It might have been better," he murmured, "to leave Andy ashore."

"I told him I wanted him here. But then he asked why we couldn't have had a day...just the two of us together..."

"I can relate to that." With the tip of his index finger, he caressed a spot just below her ear. He heard a soft in-hiss of breath. Was she feeling the same desire he was? Did she want him, as much as he wanted her?

Hell, he'd wanted her from the moment she'd sashayed into Elsa's yard weeks ago, in that sexy black getup! But that had been lust. Much more than lust was involved now.

After what Alix had said last night, he'd had to reevaluate his feelings for Meg Stafford. Had had to reach right inside himself, and lay the truth bare.

And what he'd discovered had knocked him sprawling. Alix was right. He *had* fallen in love with Meg. Wildly, crazily, and terminally. But what was he going to do about it? The woman had sworn she wasn't into commitment!

Go after her. That's what Alix had said. Go after her, Sam.

"Meg, will you have dinner with me tonight?" His tone was urgent. "I need to talk to you."

Because she'd turned her head away, he couldn't see her expression...but he'd felt her body stiffen. In rejection? Dammit, she was going to turn him down. He readied himself to work on her, pull out all the stops...

Go down on his creaky old knees if necessary.

But as it turned out, he was spared that exercise.

Turning, she fixed him with a steady gaze. "Thank you, Sam," she said. "Yes, I'll have dinner with you tonight."

CHAPTER ELEVEN

MEG knew exactly what Sam wanted to talk to her about, and she dreaded the emotional evening that lay ahead. But in the meantime she managed to hide her inner turmoil, and when Sam produced three fishing rods, she accepted one cheerily.

They all fished for over an hour but met with no luck. Meg had just laughingly suggested they give up and open a can of beans when Andy caught a beautiful salmon.

Unable to hide his initial spontaneous delight, he swiftly reverted to his former sullenness.

Meg wanted to shake him. She managed to refrain.

"I'll clean it," she said with a forced smile, and taking the fish from him, made for the companionway.

As she was going down below, she heard Sam say to Andy, "How about you try for another? One for the Matlocks?"

"No way! When are we going back in?"

"Not for a while yet." Sam's tone was as friendly as Andy's had been surly. "After your mother guts the fish, I'll grill it and we'll eat." He added quietly, "You haven't coiled that rope and put it away yet, Andy. Do it now, please, before there's an accident."

Meg moved round the tiny galley. She'd hung her shirt on a knob behind the sink earlier; she pushed it aside now before turning on the tap. This outing, she reflected, had been a *huge* mistake. After weeks of being cool but polite, Andy was once again acting with open hostility to Sam. She decided to talk to him about it as soon as possible.

She'd just finished cleaning the fish when she heard Sam's heavy tread on the companionway steps.

"Cook reporting for duty." He ducked his head as he came into the galley. "You can take a break now."

She made to slip past him, but they got jammed in the narrow space between sink and bulkhead.

Life jacket to life jacket. Face to face.

"I've said it before and I'll say it again." Lazy amusement laced Sam's voice. "You and I really have to stop bumping into each other like this!"

Well, Alix will surely put a stop to it even if we don't, Meg thought. "Let me by, Sam—"

"What's your hurry?"

"I'm going to have it out with Andy."

"Have what out?"

"He's being *so* rude to you. I'm not going to put up with it." She tried to concentrate on her words and ignore his disturbing closeness. Did *any* other man in the world have such a tempting mouth? Such seductive eyes? "I won't tolerate having him treat you as if you were guilty of some wrong. If anyone was at fault I was, for not telling you—"

"It's not about that, Meg. He knows you acted from the best of intentions. What this is about now is *sharing*. He's had you all to himself and he doesn't want that to change—but dammit, Meg, I can't stand to see you so unhappy!"

I wouldn't be so unhappy if I hadn't seen you and Alix last night, in each other's arms. "He may not want things to change and I know I can't expect him to love to order. But I can and do expect that he treat you with *respect*."

"OK. Want me to come up...for moral support?"

"No, thanks. I can manage."

He whisked her shirt from the knob and thrust it at her. "Put that on. I don't want to see you get burned."

The concern in his eyes brought a lump to her throat. She wanted to cry that it was too late; she was already burned. She'd been too close to the flame. His flame.

She swallowed over the raw lump. "Thanks." Ducking past him, she scrambled up the steps, desperate to escape before he saw her welling tears. She didn't want Andy to see them, either. She decided it would be best to go sit alone on the foredeck till she got a grip of herself again.

Andy wondered if he'd ever hated himself more.

Staring grimly down at the water, he struggled to get his anguished thoughts in order.

He wished he'd never given in to the temptation to eavesdrop on Sam Grainger and his mother. Oh, he'd only listened for a second, but it had been enough. What he'd overheard had left him feeling sick. Sick with himself.

...What this is about now is sharing. He's had you all to himself and he doesn't want that to change—but dammit, Meg, I can't stand to see you so unhappy!

Andy brushed a hand over his eyes as his vision blurred. He'd been so wrapped up in his own feelings, he'd never once stopped to consider what he was doing to his mom. She was the last person in the world he'd want to hurt. He loved her more than anything.

And of course Sam Grainger was right about him. He *didn't* want to share. He wanted things to stay the same as they'd always been—

He watched tensely as his mother appeared, a shirt over one arm, her head bent as she undid her life jacket. He knew she must have heard him being rude to his father and he braced himself for an angry tirade.

Instead, to his surprise, she ignored him. Dropping her life jacket on the cockpit bench, she stumbled past him, clutching the shirt. Her cheeks were wet.

He stared after her as she made her way along the deck, fumbling with her shirtsleeves. "Mom, what's the—?"

The boat tilted and she reached out for the rail on the cabin roof, but before she could catch hold of it, she tripped. Tripped on the sprawl of rope he'd been told—*three times been told by his father*—to coil up and put away. She lurched forward and fell heavily onto the deck, on her face—and to his horror he heard a horrible crack as her brow hit a cleat. Bone on metal.

"Mom!" His strangled cry was muffled by the thump of a wave against the hull. He saw her get to her knees, slowly, as if stunned. But then another wave lifted the boat. The deck slanted...and tipped her sideways. Like a rag doll, she slid under the guardrail. Over the edge.

And into the water.

For one devastating moment, Andy couldn't move. Then adrenaline charged through him. He leaped into action. He grabbed the man-overboard pole with its bright orange flag. And he whirled it after her as the waves lifted her away.

"Dad!" he screamed. "Come quick! Mom's overboard!"

Sam frowned as he stared unseeingly at the salmon sizzling on the grill. How was Meg making out? Would her demand that Andy treat his father with respect be met with an icy refusal? Had Andy built up such a wall of resentment that his pride would never let him climb over it?

Sam felt a wave of grief. It was well nigh *unbearable* that this boy, this son whom he wanted to love and protect, wanted nothing to do with him.

And surely it was ironic that a pattern was here being repeated, but in reverse. He had been a son closed out by his own father; now he was a father closed out by his own son.

The latter was infinitely more painful—

"Dad! Come quick!" It was Andy's voice, shrill with panic and terror. "Mom's overboard!"

Sam's heart stopped...but the rest of him did not. He flicked off the grill and vaulted up the steps. By the time his heart had started beating again, he was up on deck.

Meg was nowhere to be seen.

One rapid glance took in the discarded life jacket. Oh, God—

"Where is she?" He ripped off his shoes.

Andy pointed out wildly over the choppy waves.

Sam saw the orange marker. Of Meg, there was no sign.

Andy was hysterically babbling about it being all his fault, he hadn't tidied away the rope, she'd tripped and cracked her head, and—

Sam threw him one stark look and then dove.

He hit the water and it hit him back with a forceful blow. He struck out toward the orange flag and as he plunged forward, he searched desperately for Meg. Fierce relief surged through him when at last he saw her blond head bob to the surface. He ploughed toward her, fighting panic when once again she disappeared. The waves were high, the strong current clawing at him, fighting him every inch of the way. Each stroke was a battle.

She reappeared, just an arm sweep away. He grabbed her as she was about to go under again.

He felt an almost disabling fear when he saw she was unconscious. Her face was ashen; her brow badly gashed.

"Oh, God..." Emotion almost closed his throat. "Hang in there, Meggie..."

He struck out for the boat, but she was a dead weight

and it seemed to take an hour to get there. Andy—looking white and terrified—helped him hoist the limp body
up onto the deck.

"Radio ahead for an ambulance," Sam ordered
hoarsely as he bent over Meg. "Start the engine. Head
for home."

And praying harder than he ever had in his life, he
began administering artificial ventilation.

Seashore didn't boast a hospital. The nearest one was at
Larch Grove, and when the ambulance whined to a halt
at the emergency entrance, the Infiniti was close behind.

Once inside, Meg was wheeled away and despite
Sam's urgent request that he and Andy be allowed to
accompany her, they were firmly directed to the waiting
room after Sam had given out the details of Meg's accident and near-drowning.

Sam's last glimpse of Meg had filled him with dread.
The lump on her forehead had swelled to the size of an
egg, and she still seemed deeply unconscious.

The waiting room was small and uninviting, with four
shabby armchairs and a table scattered with old magazines. As soon as they got there, Andy flung himself into
a chair, picked up a magazine, and immersed himself in
it.

Sam paced back and forth in the corridor outside the
open doorway. He'd wanted to talk to Andy as they'd
sped along the highway, had wanted to reassure him, but
the words just wouldn't come. His own fear made it
impossible for him to give the boy any comfort; he knew
he'd break down and that was the last thing Andy
needed, to see his father lose control.

Andy himself had been tight-lipped and withdrawn.
Sam had even begun to wonder if he'd fooled himself
into thinking the boy had screamed "Dad!" on the
boat...but in the end he knew he had not. In the heat of

the moment, Andy had cast aside his hostility, and reverted to the age-old call of child to parent.

But now that his mother was in someone else's hands, Andy was back in his previous "hostility mode." And this, Sam decided, as he cast an anguished and compassionate look at his son, was not the time to call him on it.

Andy felt his stomach roiling about, and desperately hoped he wasn't going to be sick.

He'd never forgive himself if his mom didn't make it.

It was all his fault. For weeks he'd been selfish and mean and unforgivably nasty. Apart from asking him to move some furniture a month ago, Sam Grainger had only ever asked him to do one thing: tidy away an old bit of rope. He'd deliberately ignored him...and look where it had all ended up. No wonder his father hated him now—hated him so much he couldn't even speak to him. And if his mom did come through this, she'd probably hate him, too.

What a mess he'd made of everything.

He *wanted* to try to make it right. But every time he plucked up the courage to go over and apologize to his father, his throat got all choked up and he knew if he spoke, he'd cry. And what kind of a kid would his dad think him, if he saw him blubbering like a baby! So he'd taken this magazine, and buried himself in it.

He focused his gaze on the page before him...and with a sense of dismay, noticed he'd been holding it upside down!

Had his father noticed? He jerked his head up...to see his dad leaning against the wall across the way, his head bowed. Desperately Andy wanted to get up, go over to him, talk to him, tell him how sorry he was...

Do it!

He slipped the magazine onto the table, grasped the

arms of the chair, and started to get up. But even as he did, he felt tears well up, felt his throat close.

He sagged down into the chair again. It was no use.

And besides, he couldn't bear it, just couldn't bear it, if he did apologize and his dad looked at him that way again...that way he'd looked on the boat, just before he dove into the water.

Sam was slumped against the doorjamb when he saw a doctor striding along the corridor toward the waiting room.

He straightened abruptly.

The doctor stopped in front of him. "You're Mr. Stafford?" Brown eyes glinted behind wire-rimmed glasses.

"I'm Sam Grainger, a close friend." Sam beckoned Andy over. "And this is our son Andy." Sam could feel the boy's tension, as tightly drawn as his own. "How...is she?"

"Skull X rays show no sign of a fracture, but she's concussed, and I've had to stitch that gash on her brow—"

Sam slashed an impatient hand in the air. *"Is she going to be OK?"*

"I would say, cautiously, that she is. She's just regained consciousness—"

"Thank God!"

"—But she's very groggy. We'll keep her overnight, and I want her to have absolute rest."

"May we see her?" Sam asked.

"One of you may go in, but just for a minute. Tomorrow, all being well, she can go home."

Sam sent up a silent prayer of thanks. Meg was going to be OK. He released a breath he hadn't been aware he was holding. He turned to Andy.

"In you go, son. Go visit your mom."

To his surprise, he saw Andy's face crumple, the blue eyes fill with tears. ''No, you go. You're the one she'll want to see.'' He turned away. ''This is all my fault.'' His voice shook. ''If I hadn't been so—''

Sam took his shoulders and turned him gently. He felt tears flash in his own eyes when he saw the misery in his son's face. ''Andy, your mom loves you more than anyone in the world. You go on in now, and tell her how much you love her, too. That's going to make her feel better far quicker than any medicine the doctor can give her.''

Tears spilled over and rolled down Andy's face. He lurched against Sam, and put his arms around his father. Burying his face against Sam's chest, he whispered, ''I'm sorry, Dad. I'm sorry for everything...''

Sam thought his heart was going to burst. He put his arms around his son and held him tight. ''I know.'' His voice was thick with emotion. ''I know, and it's all right. Everything's going to be all right now...''

From behind him, he heard the doctor say, with a hint of resignation in his tone, ''OK, you can both go in. But one at a time. And just for a minute. So...who's first?''

Sam gave Andy a gentle shove. ''Off you go, son. Do it.''

Andy swiped his forearm across his eyes, and gave his father a tremulous smile. His eyes were still shiny, but they had a sparkle they hadn't had before. ''OK. Thanks, Dad. And I'll tell Mom you'll be coming in next.''

Meg's head felt as if someone had swung her against a wall and smashed her skull to smithereens. Eyes closed, she rode the pain, even as she heard the nurse say, ''You'll feel better in a minute or so, once the medication begins to take effect.''

Through the pain, she struggled to remember what had

happened. She'd been down in the galley with Sam, and she'd told him she was going on deck to talk with Andy. According to the nurse, she'd hurt her head and then fallen overboard and Sam had saved her, but she had no recollection—

"Mom?"

She opened her eyes and saw Andy. He was crying.

Her heart twisted. It was *years* since she'd seen Andy cry. She dug an elbow into the mattress, and ignoring the splintering agony in her head, put an arm out.

Their hug was close and emotion-filled. When she sank back on the pillows, exhausted, he said, in a choked voice, "Mom, I'm sorry. Sorry about having been such a jerk...and sorry about...this. I was careless. About the rope..."

"I don't remember..."

"I didn't coil it up and put it away like I was told. You tripped, and then you were heaved overboard by this big wave."

"Oh, Andy, we all make mistakes. The important thing is that we learn from them." She reached up and touched his tear-damp cheek. "Are you OK now?"

He nodded. She saw his throat work convulsively. "I can't stay, the doc said just a quick visit—"

"Where's...your father?"

His eyes filled with tears again. "I wanted him to come in first," he said. "But he...Dad...made me. I'll go get him now. Take care, Mom." He gave her a quick kiss and she smelled the tang of the sea on his skin. "Love you."

"Love you, too, baby."

Meg sagged back on her pillow after he left. *Dad.* So...he and his father had made their peace. She didn't know how it had happened but it filled her with joy—

"Meg...?"

Sam stood in the doorway, his face pale, his eyes dark with worry. She was shaken by his gaunt appearance.

He pulled a chair across to the bed and sat down so that he was close to her. He took her hands, held them in his. His fingers were warm and firm. His touch sent tingles of longing dancing through her.

"How are you, Meggie?"

She realized that the sedative was beginning to work. "I feel...drowsy. They gave me something, it's taking the edge off the pain." She drifted her sleepy gaze over him, taking in the dampness of his wrinkled shirt, the salty stiffness of his hair—the beautiful structure of his face, the dark forest green of his eyes. Loving him. Adoring him. "Sam...will you...look after Andy..."

"Of course."

"Thank you." She felt herself drifting away, the sensation lovely...like floating on a cloud.

He brushed a tender lingering kiss over her lips. She closed her eyes, let herself absorb the gentleness of it.

"We'll come back tomorrow."

She murmured, wanted to whisper "Yes," but no words came. She was floating away, away from him, away from everything. Just before she sank into oblivion she thought she heard him say something...but told herself she must have been dreaming.

For what she'd *thought* he said was, "I love you, Meg."

CHAPTER TWELVE

"DON'T fuss!" Meg smiled as she looked up at Sam and Andy, who were hovering around her in the sitting room. From the moment they'd brought her home from hospital an hour before, they hadn't given her a moment's peace. She shooshed Sam away as he adjusted the pillow behind her on the long sofa. "I'm not an invalid. I just feel a bit groggy. By tomorrow I'll be right as rain and back at work."

"No way!" Andy scowled at her. "Dad says you're to take the whole of next week off."

Meg rolled her eyes as she saw Sam's wide grin. They were ganging up on her. And she didn't really feel up to arguing...but if she felt like going to work, let them just try to stop her!

The phone rang through in the kitchen and Andy said, "I'll get it, it'll be Mike."

He left the room and shut the door behind him.

It was the first time she and Sam had been alone together since yesterday. She felt, suddenly, shy.

He sat down in the armchair opposite, and leaned forward, forearms set on his powerful thighs. "Meg, Andy and I went for a walk on the beach this morning before we picked you up, and we were talking—"

"I'm so glad you and he are getting along now. If nothing else good came out of my accident, this did!"

"That boy—" Sam looked at her steadily "—wants a family more than anything in the world. A family with...both a mom and a dad..."

Fear grabbed Meg by the throat. Here it was, then; what she'd been expecting, what she'd been dreading.

She held her breath as she waited for him to put it into words.

"Meg...so do I."

Alix and Sam were getting back together.

She twined her hands together on her lap. Tightly. She hadn't realized that she'd still been hoping, till this moment, that she'd been wrong. Now she struggled with all her might to accept what was going to happen.

For the past twelve years, she and Andy had been a twosome. But he was at an age now where he would forge a deep bond with his father—and that was as it should be.

Over the past weeks, she had prepared herself for this change in their situation; what she hadn't anticipated then was that Andy would become part of a new family; a family consisting of himself, his father...and a step-mother.

Inevitably, as the years went by, she would be increasingly on the outside. A pathetic, lonely figure.

"Meg, Andy slept over at the inn last night..."

She braced herself for what was to come: Sam was going to suggest that from now on Andy live at the inn, with him. Andy would initially be torn; he was a loyal kid. But he would, inevitably, choose to live with his father—and Alix, when she was there. Had Andy met her already? If so, he'd surely have been awed by her; and would find his mother dull in comparison. Meg willed back the tears that pricked her eyes; if there was one thing she *detested,* it was self-pity. "Yes, you told me. Thanks so much for looking after him."

"Meg, I want to look after you both." Sam leaned closer. "Would you be interested in coming to live at the inn, too?"

The suggestion took her completely by surprise. "But this is my home, Sam!" Did he expect her to sell it? Move into staff quarters? Deborah had had a suite in the staff quarters at the inn; it had been redecorated and now lay empty. Did Sam envisage her living there?

Her head started to pound. She winced, and touched her fingertips to the white bandage on her forehead.

Sam cursed softly and rose from his seat.

"Meg, I'm sorry. I should be letting you rest." He leaned over and adjusted the light blanket covering her. "I'll rustle up some lunch, and then you can have a nap. I have to go back to the inn for a couple of hours."

To see Alix, of course. Sam wasn't aware she knew his ex-wife had come to the inn. She should confess that she—

The door opened and Andy popped his head around. "Mom, Mike asked me to come over and keep him company. Can I go?"

Sam said, "Could you ask him for a rain check? I have to go to the inn, and I'd like you to stay here, look after your mother."

Meg expected a protest. Instead, Andy said, "Sure, Dad, no problem. Can I just nip over there, though, and pick up a game he promised to loan me?"

"Go ahead."

With a grin at his father, Andy took off again.

"I'll make your lunch now, Meg." Sam went out, too.

Meg sank back against the pillows, feeling limp and wretched, and had just closed her eyes when the door opened again.

"Oh, Meg, maybe I didn't make myself clear. When I asked you to move to the inn…I meant as my wife. Think it over, will you? And let me know what you decide."

Sam's hands were deft and competent as he whisked eggs for the omelette he was making—but his mind was spinning out of control. He couldn't believe what he'd just done.

He'd proposed marriage to Meg.

And then, like the coward he was, he'd fled.

He laughed dryly. Imagine that—he'd been afraid to hang around, because he didn't have the courage to watch her face as she assimilated what she'd just heard. A proposal of marriage to a woman who loved her life *exactly* as it was.

He must have been crazy to think she'd ever—

"Sam?"

He dropped the fork as her voice came from the kitchen doorway, and it clattered to the floor.

He ignored it.

Turning, he stared at the ashen-cheeked woman standing looking back at him, one hand against the doorjamb to brace herself. Her blue eyes were stark, her lips trembling.

"Meg." He walked quickly over to her. "Honey, you should be lying down. Let me take you back to the—"

She placed her free hand on his chest and stopped him. "Sam…" Her voice wobbled. "Was I hearing things?"

"No." His smile was wry. "No, you weren't."

"You…want to marry me?"

"Yeah."

"But…what about Alix?"

He blinked, looked bewildered. "What the hell does Alix have to do with this?"

"Sam, I have a…confession to make. I…came to see you…on Friday night, to ask why you'd been so…aloof all week, and I was passing your sitting room window and I…heard…saw you…with Alix…she was in your arms—"

He opened his mouth to speak but she rushed on. "Before I ran away, I heard her say that now you have Andy, your marriage would work because—"

He pressed his fingertips gently to her mouth to stop her from going on. "If you had waited," he said, "you'd have heard me tell her, as I did when I broke up with her, that our marriage was over for good. I meant it then, and I meant it on Friday night. Do you believe me?''

Meg felt giddy, disorientated. ''Where…is Alix now?''

''Gone.'' Just one word, but his eyes were repeating the question he'd already asked, Do you believe me?

''Yes,'' she whispered. ''I believe you.''

''So…will you marry me, Meggie, dear?''

She swallowed a few times, and then cleared a huskiness from her throat. ''Do you want a…marriage of convenience?''

She meant, of course, did he want to marry her because of Andy; to give Andy his name. To live together in a platonic relationship. That kind of a marriage—a marriage of convenience—was the *last* thing he wanted…but heck, he had a foot in the door, he wasn't about to have her slam it on him while there was still hope. Hope for more.

''If that's what *you* want.'' What *he* wanted, right now, was to sweep her up in his arms and carry her back to the sofa. She looked all in. Her hair was mussed, her eyes slightly bloodshot, her brow, under the bandage, so very swollen. And in those dusty pink sweats Andy had brought to her in the hospital, she looked so fragile a gust of wind could surely blow her over. He'd said he wanted to look after her; what he hadn't told her was—he loved her. He hadn't had the courage.

But the courage would come. He hoped!

''It…wouldn't work.'' A tear trembled on the lower lid of her left eye. She dropped her hand from the doorjamb and turned to go. Her shoulders drooped disconsolately. She swayed a little.

In a heartbeat, Sam was doing what he'd wanted to do a moment ago—sweep her up into his arms. ''You need to lie down,'' he said. ''You can't cope with this right now. We'll talk later.''

She dropped her head against his chest. ''It's no use.''

Her voice was muffled. "There's no use putting it off, nothing's going to change. I can't change how I *feel*."

He paused, and looked down at her. All he could see was the crown of her head, and the tousled dazzle of white gold. He heard a faint sound, and to his dismay, he realized she was crying.

Sliding a finger under her chin, he tipped her face up. "Meggie…how *do* you feel?" he asked.

He braced himself for a rejection. She would never be unkind, not deliberately unkind…

But she didn't know he was in love with her.

She looked up at him through lashes wet with tears. "Oh, Sam," she said brokenly, "do you really not know? I've been crazy about you for as long as I can remember. There's no way I could marry you…knowing you don't feel the same way about me!"

He almost dropped her. "You're…in *love* with me?"

Her shaky chuckle was embarrassed. "Daft, isn't it?"

He closed his eyes, and was almost afraid to open them again, in case he'd been dreaming. But no—when he opened them again, she was still there. Still looking up at him with that forlorn, lovelorn expression.

He smiled, a slowly forming smile that creased his face and reached deep, deep into his eyes. "Then if you're daft, Meggie mine, I'm daft, too! I've been yours for the taking from the moment you sashayed into Elsa's backyard in that sexy black getup, but I've been so wrapped up in my own disillusionment, it's taken me all this time to admit it!"

"Oh, Sam." She smiled up at him blissfully. "I really did hear it last night, then?"

"Hear what?"

"After you kissed me, I heard you say you loved me…but afterward, I thought I must have dreamed it."

"That was no dream." He kissed her, just as he had last night, but even more thoroughly. Her lips were dry and she smelled of antiseptic, but the kiss was the sweetest he had ever known. "It's real, sweetheart…and it's forever."

"Sam…" Her eyes were troubled. "…There's just one thing. I…know you love Andy…but he's a grown boy. May I ask you a question—just tell me, if I'm out of line…"

"Nothing you could ask me could ever be out of line!" Kissing her again, he carried her to the sitting room and deposited her carefully on the couch.

"Now—" he sat on the edge of the middle cushion, facing her "—what's this question you think may offend me?"

"What do you have against babies?"

"What makes you think I've anything against babies? I love babies…adore them, as a matter of fact!"

"But then—" She bit her lip hesitantly. "Why didn't you and Alix have any?"

He took both her hands in his. "Before we became engaged, Alix told me she loved kids, and that once we were married, she wanted to get pregnant right away. So as soon as we were married, we tried…but no luck. After a couple of years, she said she'd go to her gynecologist, get him to run some tests. She reported back to me that he'd told her there was no reason for her not to have a family."

"So then…you got checked out?"

"Yup, I went to my own doc, got the all clear, too."

"Then you must have both been encouraged, all you had to do was…keep trying."

"We did keep trying, but no luck. After another couple of years, I suggested adopting, but Alix wasn't interested. I couldn't argue with her…and didn't. That kind of a decision, that kind of commitment, needs to be unanimous."

"And was it because…of the stress, the continuing disappointment, that you broke up?"

"No." His eyes became hard. "I found out, by

chance—just over a year ago—that Alix had lied to me. Had been lying to me all along. I'd never met her gyne man, but I bumped into him one day at a business lunch. We got to talking, I asked him if he had family, he said a wife and three daughters. Then he said he and his wife had always wanted children, but he could respect those who didn't and who did something about it...like Alix, he added, getting her tubes tied before we got married because we had both agreed we didn't want kids.''

For a long moment, Meg's face was blank. Then as understanding dawned, horror widened her gaze. She looked at him with an anguished expression.

''You mean...she...all these years, when you were trying to have a family, she knew it was *impossible*?''

He nodded. ''When I found out, it was the end of the marriage. It was the oddest thing,'' he added, almost to himself. ''My love for her just...died. Because she wasn't the person I'd thought she was, but...a stranger.''

''Oh, Sam.'' Meg's voice came out chokingly as she pulled herself up. ''What an unforgivable betrayal.'' She threw her arms around him, and in a moment he felt her tears seep through his shirt. She sobbed for a while, and when the sobs started to subside, she pulled back, and looked up at him through her tears.

''Sweetheart,'' she whispered, ''I love babies, too. I never thought I'd have another, but now...''

''Now things are different.'' He framed her face in his hands. ''And we're going to have to move on this project fast. Hell, I'm going to be forty next week!''

''You're in your prime, Sam Grainger.'' Meg's smile was watery but adoring. ''But I agree, we should get started on this right away.''

''Started on what?'' Andy's voice came from the doorway. ''What am I missing?''

Arms around each other, they turned to face him.

''What you're missing,'' Sam said, ''are siblings. And

your mother and I are just arranging to rectify that omission at the first possible opportunity!''

Andy grinned through a rising blush. ''Hey, you shouldn't be talking like that, not in front of innocent kids. I'm outta here!''

They heard him chuckling as he walked away.

''With that boy popping in and out all the time,'' Sam grumbled, ''we're going to have to behave ourselves. At least, till we get married!''

''Then we'll have to get married soon!'' Meg said fervently. ''How about a Christmas wedding, at the inn. A quiet wedding. And for our honeymoon—''

''I guess you want to fly to somewhere hot and exotic! The Caribbean? Spain? Hawaii?''

She linked her fingers at his nape. ''No,'' she said. ''Where I want to go, we'll have to wrap up well, take lots of blankets, and a humungous thermos of hot chocolate.''

''Alaska? Iceland? The Arctic?''

She laughed, but a shy blush drifted up over her face. ''Under the madrona tree. I want us to start over, where all this began. I want you to love me the way you did that night, so you can share my wonderful memories. Under that tree was a special place for me.'' Her blush deepened. ''I've never told you this, Sam, but...you were...the first.''

Sam took in a shaky breath. He'd always meant to ask, but it had been easy not to. He hadn't wanted to hear the answer. Now, though, it was different. Now he could spend the rest of his life making it up to her. And he would...

''I love you, Meggy mine,'' he whispered against her lips.

''I love you, too, Sam Grainger!''

And after that, there was no need for words.

MILLS & BOON®

Makes any time special

Enjoy a romantic novel from
Mills & Boon®

Presents™ *Enchanted*™ *Temptation*®

Historical Romance™ *Medical Romance*™

MILLS & BOON®

Next Month's Romance Titles

♡

Each month you can choose from a wide variety of romance novels from Mills & Boon®. Below are the new titles to look out for next month from the Presents™ and Enchanted™ series.

Presents™

THE SPANISH GROOM	Lynne Graham
HER GUILTY SECRET	Anne Mather
THE PATERNITY AFFAIR	Robyn Donald
MARRIAGE ON THE EDGE	Sandra Marton
THE UNEXPECTED BABY	Diana Hamilton
VIRGIN MISTRESS	Kay Thorpe
MAKESHIFT MARRIAGE	Daphne Clair
SATURDAY'S BRIDE	Kate Walker

Enchanted™

AN INNOCENT BRIDE	Betty Neels
NELL'S COWBOY	Debbie Macomber
DADDY AND DAUGHTERS	Barbara McMahon
MARRYING WILLIAM	Trisha David
HIS GIRL MONDAY TO FRIDAY	Linda Miles
BRIDE INCLUDED	Janelle Denison
OUTBACK WIFE AND MOTHER	Barbara Hannay
HAVE BABY, WILL MARRY	Christie Ridgway

On sale from 7th May 1999

H1 9904

Available at most branches of WH Smith, Tesco, Asda, Martins, Borders, Easons, Volume One/James Thin and most good paperback bookshops

MILLS & BOON®

Medical Romance™

COMING NEXT MONTH

VILLAGE PARTNERS by Laura MacDonald

Dr Sara Denton tried to forget Dr Alex Mason, but it didn't work. Then she went to her uncle's and found Alex was a partner at the general practice! And Alex *really* wanted her to stay...

ONE OF A KIND by Alison Roberts

Dr Sam Marshall, fresh from Australia, was certainly unique! Sister Kate Campbell, with an A&E department to run at the busy London hospital, had no time to spare, but Sam was persistent!

MARRYING HER PARTNER by Jennifer Taylor
A Country Practice—the first of four books.

Dr Elizabeth Allen wasn't comfortable with change, but when Dr James Sinclair arrived at the Lake District practice, change was inevitable!

ONE OF THE FAMILY by Meredith Webber

Nurse Sarah Tremaine wanted to adopt baby Sam, but first she had to get permission from the child's uncle. But Dr Adam Fletcher didn't know he had a nephew...

Available from 7th May 1999

Available at most branches of WH Smith, Tesco, Asda, Martins, Borders, Easons, Volume One/James Thin and most good paperback bookshops

4 FREE

books and a surprise gift!

We would like to take this opportunity to thank you for reading this Mills & Boon® book by offering you the chance to take FOUR more specially selected titles from the Enchanted™ series absolutely FREE! We're also making this offer to introduce you to the benefits of the Reader Service™—

- ★ FREE home delivery
- ★ FREE gifts and competitions
- ★ FREE monthly Newsletter
- ★ Exclusive Reader Service discounts
- ★ Books available before they're in the shops

Accepting these FREE books and gift places you under no obligation to buy, you may cancel at any time, even after receiving your free shipment. Simply complete your details below and return the entire page to the address below. *You don't even need a stamp!*

YES! Please send me 4 free Enchanted books and a surprise gift. I understand that unless you hear from me, I will receive 6 superb new titles every month for just £2.40 each, postage and packing free. I am under no obligation to purchase any books and may cancel my subscription at any time. The free books and gift will be mine to keep in any case.

N9EA

Ms/Mrs/Miss/Mr ....Initials..............................
BLOCK CAPITALS PLEASE

Surname ....

Address ....

....

....Postcode..............................

Send this whole page to:
THE READER SERVICE, FREEPOST CN81, CROYDON, CR9 3WZ
(Eire readers please send coupon to: P.O. BOX 4546, DUBLIN 24.)

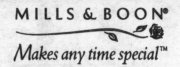

MILLS & BOON®

Makes any time special™

The Regency Collection

Mills & Boon® is delighted to bring back, for a limited period, 12 of our favourite Regency Romances for you to enjoy.

These special books will be available for you to collect each month from May, and with two full-length Historical Romance™ novels in each volume they are great value at only £4.99.

Volume One available from 7th May